Red Butterfly

Red Butterfly

A. L. Sonnichsen

ILLUSTRATED BY Amy June Bates

SIMON & SCHUSTER
BOOKS FOR YOUNG READERS

NEW YORK LONDON TORONTO SYDNEY NEW DELHI

SIMON & SCHUSTER BOOKS FOR YOUNG READERS
An imprint of Simon & Schuster Children's Publishing Division
1230 Avenue of the Americas, New York, New York 10020

Book design by Laurent Linn
The text for this book is set in Arrus Std.
Manufactured in the United States of America
0115 FFG
2 4 6 8 10 9 7 5 3 1
Library of Congress Cataloging-in-Publication Data
Sonnichsen, A. L.
Red butterfly / A. L. Sonnichsen.—First edition.
pages cm
Summary: In China, a foundling girl with a deformed hand raised in secret by an American woman must navigate China's strict adoption system when she is torn away from the only family she has ever known.
ISBN 978-1-4814-1109-7 (hardcover : alk. paper)
ISBN 978-1-4814-1111-0 (eBook)
[1. Novels in verse. 2. Families—Fiction. 3. Intercountry adoption—Fiction. 4. Adoption—Fiction. 5. Foundlings—Fiction. 6. Abnormalities, Human—Fiction. 7. China—Fiction.] I. Title.
PZ7.5.S67Re 2015
[Fic]—dc23
2013050300
FIRST EDITION

For Olivia

Part One

Crawl

Mama's Piano

Mama used to have a piano
with an on/off switch
and a dial to make drums beat.

It stood on metal legs
next to the window
that looks across at
rows of other apartments,
with tiled paths
edged in concrete planters below.

Mama would sit on a stool,
crack the window
to let in the outside air
as she played
from memory,
eyes closed,
shoulders straight,
body swaying
forward and back,

as if she were a tree
bending in a slow breeze,
as if her fingers were leaves
tapping sounds into the air.

We sold that piano
because food
became more important
than music.

Now, two years later,
Mama's fingers can only
run over the edge of the tabletop,
remembering what it was like to be free.

To Market

Mama sends me
for leafy, green
qingcai today
because she prefers it
over cabbage.

She'll fry it
with a little oil,
salt,
and garlic
from the garlic braid
hanging from the
oil-sticky
kitchen window.

Then we'll eat
at the fold-out table
with the peeling top
and Mama will chew
slowly
because her teeth hurt.

I take
one thin blue note
from the food envelope
in Mama's drawer
while she goes over our rules:
Don't talk too much,
but be pleasant,
not afraid.
Don't chat with strangers
or tell them
where you live.

She doesn't need to tell me.
The rules are natural.
They seal me in
like a second skin.
I could not behave differently
if I wanted to.

Natural

I'm used to her never leaving our apartment.

If she does, she covers herself
in a head scarf,
long gloves,
sunglasses,
collar turned up
in nighttime and in summer.

But she hardly ever leaves.

She says the China air
makes her shrivel
like a peach
left in the sun,
which may be
because she's turning
seventy soon.
She says she can see enough of China
from our sixth-floor
window,
which may be
because the stairs
make her knees creak.

But I'm not sure
if any of those
are the real reasons she stays.

Red Butterfly

I ride with my hair
whipping back,
a long,
flapping
black flag.

Wind
presses my face,
freezes my lips,
laces the cracks in my knuckles with blood.

The city
is a blur.
No one stares,
no one asks questions
when I am alone,
pedaling my ruby-red bicycle.
No one knows I am different,
    that I have an American mother,
    that even though I look Chinese,
    I'm American on the inside.

When I ride
I am like the ten million others
moving in slow motion
down frozen streets
in January.

Except I am faster,
flitting between them,
    a red butterfly.

Far-Away Eyes

Mama's eyes
yearn
for Montana,
where she was born,
raised,
married.

My older sister Jody,
who is almost
forty,
was born there,
still lives there.

My daddy
lives there too,
though he didn't always.

When I was little
he lived in China
with Mama and me,
though I don't remember much
about that,
just hugging him
the day he said good-bye.

I have pictures to prove
he was here, though—
  a thin man with a scruffy-faced
  half smile,
  holding a small me
  to his hip.
  In the picture
  I am looking up at him
  like he's the world.

Mama is thinking about Montana now
when she says,
The mountains, Kara!
Oh, if you could only see the mountains!

Tianjin, our city,
is pancake flat,
no mountains for miles.

Though I've heard
if you leave in a car

you can drive to where the Great Wall snakes
up-and-down peaks
steep as upside-down paper cones.

I've seen pictures.

Maybe I should take Mama there,
let her perch
on the back of my bicycle,
ride all the way
to the Chinese mountains
so her eyes will
return to me.

Patience

Mama says
we will go to Daddy someday,
move to America where we
will all be happy.

When you're eighteen,
Mama says,
we'll work everything out.
Just seven more years,
we'll get on a plane
cross the wide ocean,
and make our home
in the mountains.

I say,
We should go now.

Mama pats my hand
with her ropy, thin one.
Patience,
Kara dear,
everything in its time.

This is Mama's
answer
to all my questions:
she feeds me
dreams and promises
with patience required.

That's why I've mostly
stopped
asking.

The Schedule

The schedule
has been taped to our refrigerator
forever.

7 a.m. Wake up
~~7:30 a.m. Clean Chirpy's cage~~
8 a.m. Breakfast

9 a.m. Study
11 a.m. Television
12 p.m. Lunch
1 p.m. Reading
3 p.m. Errands
5 p.m. Dinner
6:30 p.m. Television
8 p.m. Sleep

We only deviate
on Sunday,
when we
sleep late,
watch extra TV,
and Mama waits till ten
to scramble eggs.

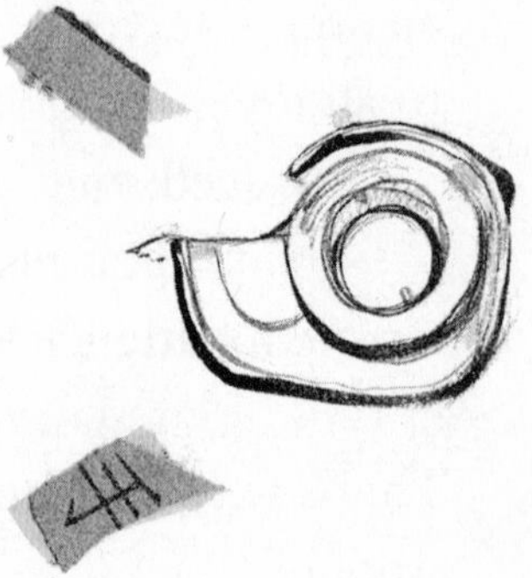

When the tape
peels
around the schedule's edges,
Mama slaps on more
so the paper
is held by so many layers
of sticky plastic
it can never
be removed.

Cage

Chirpy was my own
green bird
that lived in a
delicate cage
above Mama's piano.

He'd preen and chatter,
scatter seeds on the floor,
hop from one perch
to another,
black eyes like jewels.

I wrote Daddy a letter
and told him about Chirpy.

He wrote back,
said
Chirpy was no kind of name for a bird.
Jim was better.
Come here, Jim
Sing us a song, Jim
Polly want a cracker, Jim?

Mama promised Daddy was joking.

Then one day Jim was
gone,

just a green
tense
feather bundle
with stick legs
tipped over
on the cage bottom.

I buried him
in the garden soil
far below our
sixth-floor window,
pausing for a moment
to touch the softness
of his feathers.

Mama stashed his cage
on top of her wardrobe
in case we bought another bird
    (but we never did
    because birds
    and seeds
    cost money).

Now she stands on a chair
to tug the cage down,
finds an old blanket,
and tells me
to spread it
on the street corner.

I will sit there
until someone comes
who wants a birdcage.

Don't take any less
than twenty kuai,
Mama says.
We need at least that
to buy a phone card
to call Daddy.

I know why we need to call Daddy.
We've eaten
qingcai and cabbage
for two weeks now
and the rice in the bag only reaches
to my wrist.

Jim's cage is going
the same way
as Mama's piano—
because Daddy forgot
to send us money
to live.

Beggar

I despise
sitting

in Mama's old coat
(the sleeves
of mine
are too short)
on a holey blanket
like a beggar.

I feel as filthy
as the
sidewalk's
spots of
black
gum,
globs of
yellow
spit,
layers of
sticky
dirt.

The looks people
give me
are even dirtier.

Nobody wants
a used
birdcage.

Not even for twenty *kuai*.

Desperation

When I return
after dark
towing the unsold
birdcage,
Mama says,
Plan B,
and sends
me to borrow money from
our neighbor
Zhang Laoshi,
who's older than Mama
and bent like a witch
from the story of
Hansel and Gretel
in our Brothers Grimm.

I'm not usually
allowed
in Zhang Laoshi's
apartment
    (which is cold all winter
    and smells like
    a Chinese medicine shop)
because Mama
says Zhang Laoshi
will fill my ears with
nonsense.

Today when I knock
tentatively
on her second-floor door,
the spark of the forbidden
shivers up my arms
though I remind myself,
    Mama sent me,
    Mama sent me,
    Mama sent me.

It still feels like
all the other times
I've snuck down here
when Mama didn't know.

Zhang Laoshi's Opinion

Zhang Laoshi
gives me her opinion
on everything,
    from how much I spent on vegetables
    (always too much)
to
    how long Daddy has been gone
    (much too long).

Zhang Laoshi once told me
    it's not natural
    for a mama

to be as old
as my mama.
It's not natural
to have a sister
as old as a mother should be
or a niece and nephew
as old as me.

And I told her back:
Well, it's not natural
for a mother to leave a baby
next to the garbage drop
wrapped in a blanket
not thick enough to be a dish towel.

That stopped
Zhang Laoshi's mouth.

She is the one
who found me
when I was a newborn
wailing
in the cold.

It was Zhang Laoshi
who told Mama
I was there,
because she hoped
Mama would take me
for the night.

What she didn't plan on
was my American mama
keeping me forever.

A Visit

Zhang Laoshi
sits me in a polished-wood chair,
serves me sunflower seeds
and hot chrysanthemum tea.

Mama said to go in,
ask for the money,
and come straight back out.

Don't make conversation!

But that would feel rude.

Zhang Laoshi
leans over,
breath smelling of
garlic
and
sour candy.

Things must be getting bad,
she says.
Your father didn't send money?

We need the money
so we can call him.
An ache begins
in the back of my throat.
It's not his fault.
He works hard
and sends us
almost
all his money.
This month something
just went wrong . . .

I've said too much.
Mama would be upset
if she knew
I was down here
blabbing,
but I hate Zhang Laoshi
thinking bad thoughts
about Daddy.

She rifles through
a blue ginger jar
on a dark shelf in the corner.

As she presses fifty *kuai*
into my palm
she says,
If you're ever hungry, child,
come to me.

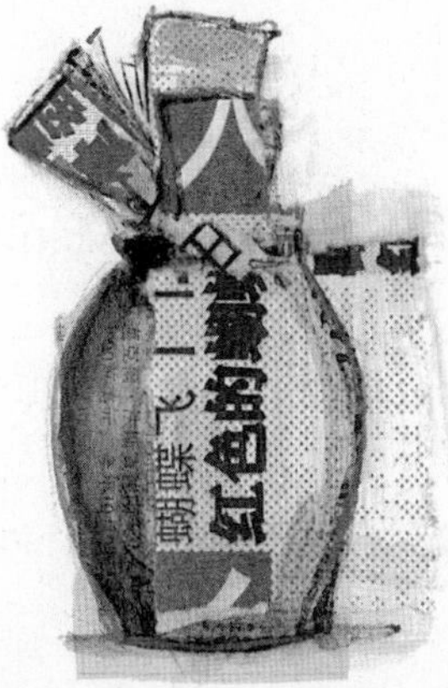

I feel her gaze rest
on my too-big coat
on my too-short jeans
on the wisp of hair that keeps trailing
into my eyes
no matter how often I breathe it away.

I tuck the money
in my sleeve
and take another
slow
sip of tea.

Mystery Words

Whenever I'm with Zhang Laoshi
she brings up the same subject:
the night Mama brought me home.

She talks about it
like it's a secret,
lowering her voice to a whisper.

Your mama has a good heart,
Zhang Laoshi says,
but even with her good heart
she made a mess.

She should have turned you over
to the police,
but she wanted to keep you.
Her heart was too big
to let you go.

It was a bad choice,
too much love,
not enough brains.

You have no /something/.
She never /something/.
Do you understand?

Those /something/ words
are missing puzzle pieces
I don't understand,

but I nod
so Zhang Laoshi's bright eyes
staring out from the folds of her
blotchy skin
won't spot my confusion.

Debt

Mama takes Zhang Laoshi's money
with a sigh.

We only asked for twenty!
Now I owe her more!

But then she softens.

You told her thank you?
How much
we appreciate
her kindness?

I nod.
Of course I did.

I only said
xie xie
a thousand times.

Reasons

According to Zhang Laoshi
the government allows
parents to have only
one child.

Second children
cost too much.

China is overrun
with people.

Boys are worth more
than girls.

Children with disease
or deformity
are worth even less.

Which
puts me
I guess
at the
very
bottom
of the barrel.

My Secret

Hidden under my long shirtsleeve
is my one blunt hand
with two short nubs
instead of fingers.

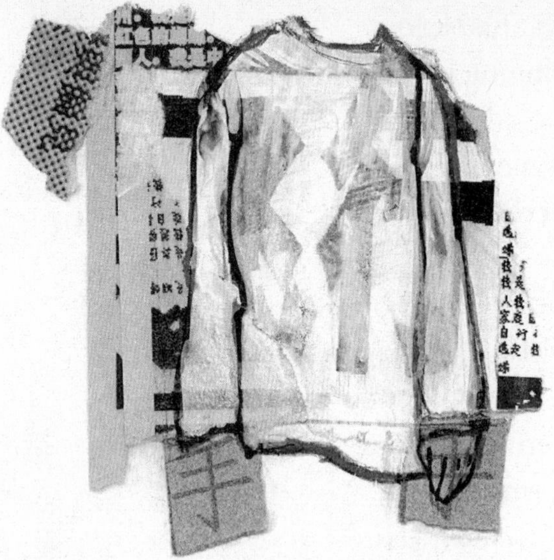

This is why my birth mother
didn't keep me,
why she decided to try again
for someone better.

Mess

I cannot use Zhang Laoshi's words
to ask Mama the questions
burning in my chest.

How will I bring them up
out of cold, blue nothing
when I have never
talked about them before?

But I want to know
why bringing me home
why not calling the police
made a mess,
why I feel the pressure
of blame
when no one has ever
blamed me aloud
    for Daddy leaving,
    for my bad Chinese,
    for our long days inside,
        Mama hiding from the sun,
        never sending me to school
        as if we were blotting out
            our own existences
        and only surviving
                day
                by
                day
                by
                day.

What is the disaster I cannot see?

Or am I the disaster
with my stubby hand?

Am I the mess no one can fix?

Bury

My fear
of upsetting
quiet
gentle
Mama
makes me
wrap up my
questions
like spoiled meat
in butcher paper
and bury them so deep,
so long,
I can almost forget they're there.

Others

I wake early
the next morning,
peek through the window
to watch the kids
from our building
leave for school.

One wears a
red scarf knotted at her throat,
climbs on the back
of her baba's motorbike.

Another
with purple hair-streaks
inspects her nails as she
waits for a taxi,
the same taxi
every day.

The only boy
in our building
has a nice mouth,
a mouth with two dimples
in either cheek.

His name is Zhao Bin.

He rides his bike alone,
his mother
shouting
warnings and
good-byes
from their third-
floor window.

Seeing him
wave over his shoulder
makes my heart stutter.

I imagine him
waving at me.

We both ride our bikes too fast.

Phone Card

Mama sends me to
buy a phone card
to call Daddy.

The woman wants one hundred,
but I haggle her down
to twenty.

She acts angry,
rummages through
her pink
fanny pack
for change,
hands me the card,
and shoos me away.

Misplaced

On my way home,
like always,
I inspect
each
passing
face,
realizing
one of them
could be
her.

I'm not sure what I'd do
if I found someone
who looked
like
me,
    walked
    like
    me,
        laughed
        like
        me.

Excuse me, ma'am,
but eleven years ago
did you
misplace a child?

Secrets

Mama and I call Daddy,
our ears pressed
to the receiver,
our foreheads touching.

Daddy can't believe
we're so low on money.
    Why didn't we call sooner?
    Are we okay?

Mama assures him we're fine,
just tired of eating cabbage.

But I sent it . . . ,
he says.

Well, I'm afraid it never came,
she says.
We need more.

Daddy is quiet.

Mama squeezes my hand.
Give us a minute,
Kara dear.

I back
into the kitchen
for a glass of water.

From the counter where I pour
I can
watch Mama
without her seeing.

She hunches over the phone,
lowers her voice to a whisper.

I was so worried,
she says, gravel-voiced.
Did you pay Mr. Wang?

I don't know who Mr. Wang is
or why
he needs to be
paid.

But their
    secrets
        make my gut crumple
        hard and tight
        like a fistful of paper.

Mama Hangs Up

She tries
to smile
but the smile
loses its way.

He's sending more money.
A kiss on my forehead
is supposed to mean
everything is okay.

But what if
this keeps happening?
I ask.
Why don't we just
go live in America
with Daddy
now?

Everything

Don't ask me,
Kara,
don't ask me.

Don't make this hard,
Kara,
don't make this harder to bear.

Be thankful,
Kara,
you have a mother,
a father,
a sister.

Be thankful,
Kara,
you have a home,
food,
safety.

Translation:
Don't ask for more,
Kara,
than what I give you,
because I'm giving you
everything.

Normal

Sometimes
I don't want everything
if this is
EVERYTHING.

Sometimes
I want normal.

Whatever that is.

Phone Call

All these weeks
the phone has been silent.
Daddy never calls,
he only writes long letters
on lined notebook paper.
Cheaper that way.

Now the phone *ring*
ring
rings

Mama leaps to answer,
suddenly as active
as a young gazelle
on a nature program.

Spring!
Spring!
Spring!

My sister Jody's voice blares
through the earpiece,
her very loud voice
that makes me cringe
because who needs to speak
so loudly
when we are right here
with our ears pressed
to the phone?

Sheesh.

I'm coming to visit,
she says.
Roll out the red carpet.

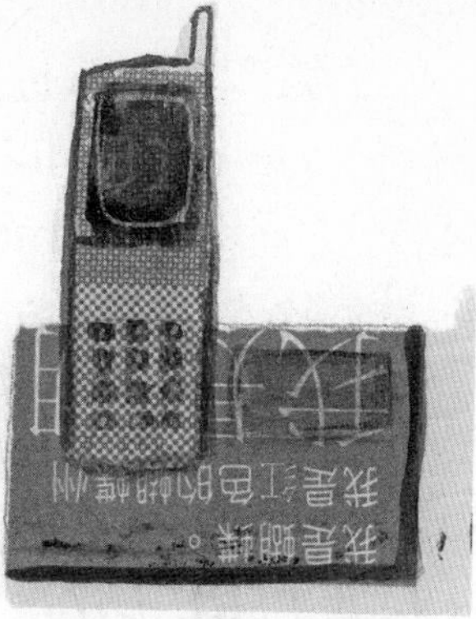

Visitors

We don't get visitors.
Jody is the only one,
and she has only come
from America twice
my whole life.

Once, before Daddy moved back to Montana,
another time two years ago
"to check on us."

That first visit is part of my
photo album of memories:
things I don't remember except for pictures
to prove they happened.
Daddy's part of that album too.

I'm on a bridge in Hangzhou
between Daddy and Jody.
Hangzhou is
the city of artists and poets,
gardens and tea.

Three years old,
that's all I was,
but Mama says we took the train there,
the train back
overnight
and it was so beautiful
I couldn't believe it.

It must have been the adventure
of our lives.

It must have been,
because Mama is standing in pictures
with her arms and face bare to the sun,
and a smile as big as a tipped half-moon.

It was sometime after that,
after Jody returned home,
that Daddy left too.

Mama tells me the reason—
Teaching English wasn't his thing,
as if that explanation should span
the nothingness
of his memory.

When it comes to Mama's husband,
my father,
all I have are crumpled letters,
old photographs,

and the times I've heard his voice
over the phone.

He never visits,
just sends Jody.
Last time she said,
Daddy sends his love
as if that makes up for everything,
especially Mama's far-away eyes
wishing for Montana.

Explaining Jody

She is loud because she lives in Montana
and must holler from
one mountain to another.

That's Mama's excuse for her.

Also, she's a reporter,
so she must make her voice heard
or no one will listen.

I know other facts about Jody:

Matthew and Madison
are the names of
her blue-eyed children
nearly my age.

She has a dog named Sparky,
taller than Madison's shoulder.
(I wonder how you fit a dog
THAT BIG
in your apartment?)

A husband named Willard
I've never met,
haven't even seen pictures of
because he's camera shy.

In their apartment
is a thing called a fireplace
where you burn trees
and hang socks for Santa
at Christmastime.

This is where
Jody,
Matthew,
Madison,
and Sparky
take family pictures.

Minus Willard.

The Last Time

The last time
Jody came
everything was
discombobulated

and expensive.

Jody wanted
fancy food,
fancy drinks,
and wanted
Mama to pay for it all.

After she left
we ate cabbage
and rice
for a month
even though Daddy
sent extra money.

Mama doesn't understand
why I'm not more excited about
Jody coming.

She's your sister,
she says.

I'm already sick of cabbage,
I say.

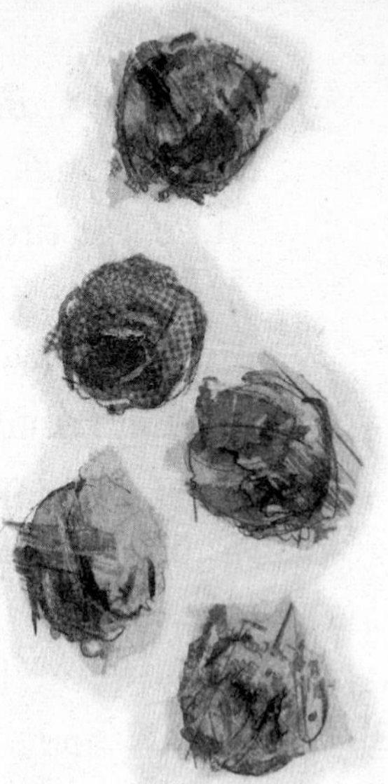

She knits
her invisible eyebrows
together
and won't try to figure out
what I mean.

Jody is her daughter
born out of her body.
    I guess I shouldn't expect Mama
    to understand.
She's probably excited
to have someone to talk to
    besides me.

Zhao Bin

I am going down,
he is going up
at three fifteen p.m.
on a Saturday.

I am going out to free time,
    to ride my bike,
    to buy vegetables.
He is coming back
    from Saturday
    half-day school.

He only moved here one year ago
and he has never come up
at three fifteen p.m. on a Saturday
when I'm going down.

It is strange to see him up close
after only watching him
from the window.

His mouth turns up
when he sees me
and the dimples appear
when he smiles.

I try to do it back,
that easy smile,
but my heart distracts me,
hurling itself against
the cage of my chest
like it wants to
break out
and scurry away.

Regular Family

I learned his name,
Zhao Bin,
from listening to his mother
yell at him.

All the family's voices
curl out into
the echoing stairwell:
    Father
    Mother
    Grandmother
    Grandfather
    Zhao Bin

Usually
when I pass,
I slow down,
every step a
tiny
soundless
centimeter
so I can
listen to their
quick
comfortable
chatter
through the
iron
gate.

I secretly wish,
even when they call
Zhao Bin
stupid boy
because of his mistakes,

that I could be part of
a regular family
like theirs.

Jody's Visit

Mama counts the days
on a calendar,
crossing them out in
    thick
    black
    pen.

Jody is coming in June,
now it is February.
    A lot of counting.

I wish Daddy would visit
instead of loud Jody.
I wrote to ask him,
but he wrote back:
    The old savings account can't take
    that kind of abuse,
    not as long as I'm working security,
    and I've got a feeling
    my days of long-distance travel are over.
    I'm not as tough as your mama.
    My old back . . .

Then he drew a round
smiling face
with one eye closed.

I guess a ticket to China is so expensive,
only rich reporters like Jody can afford one.

My Idea

I write back to Daddy
with an idea.

Mama says it's rude to ask for things
for oneself,
so I don't show her the letter before I
paste on the stamps.

Mama has books
in storage
in Montana,
old ones
from when she was young:
    a Jane Austen box set
    and one about a girl
    who finds secret tunnels
    and solves mysteries.
Nobody's looked at them in twenty years.

If Daddy can't come himself,
can he please let Jody bring the books?

I mail the letter
while I'm out buying vegetables,
ride my bike
extra fast
to the post office and back.
In all the excitement
I left my gloves at home.
Icy wind carves blood-patterns
on my knuckles,
but thinking of all those words
in hiding
waiting to be read
makes my brain fizzy,
my heart warm.

At home,
I crack open the copy of *Jane Eyre*
I've already read
seven times.

Anticipation
makes every word new.

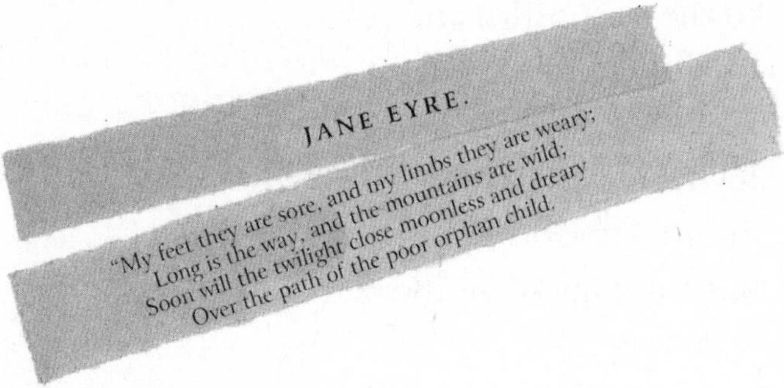
JANE EYRE.
"My feet they are sore, and my limbs they are weary;
Long is the way, and the mountains are wild;
Soon will the twilight close moonless and dreary
Over the path of the poor orphan child.

Dreams

Ninety days
until Jody comes
and all I can think of
is Mama's Jane Austen box set.

If Jody would bring
Mama's Jane Austen box set,
I would forgive Daddy
for never coming.

If Jody would bring
Mama's Jane Austen box set,

I will never
think bad thoughts
ever
again
about my scheduled,
going-nowhere
life.

Bozeman

No,
Mama says,
we can't ask Jody
for the Jane Austen box set.

It's in Bozeman
with Daddy
and she's in Missoula
with Matthew,
Madison,
the big dog, Sparky,
and Willard.

Bozeman
and
Missoula
are
mountains
and

mountains
and
mountains
apart.

We can't ask such a thing.
It would be an
in
con
ven
ience.

(I don't tell her I already asked

a month ago.)

Distance

I thought
Bozeman
and
Missoula
were two places
in the same place.

I thought
you could
pedal a bicycle
and be there in
half an hour.

But I guess
Montana is like
Jane Eyre's England:
you can walk forever
and still not be
where you want to go.

And I guess
this means
I won't be getting
Jane Austen
because Daddy can't be expected
to go that far
for me.

Trapped

What would it be like
to take my red bicycle
and ride
ride
ride
forever?

I wonder if I could reach
the snaking Great Wall
or Hangzhou with
its gardens and bridges
or the place where the ocean
sloshes onto the land.

But all I know
is this small section
of neighborhood,
this tiny corner
of a huge city.

Even though
Mama says
it's bigger than
any city in America,
    I still feel trapped.

School Time

At nine a.m.
Mama says,
School time!
loud and cheerful like always,
pretending this is exciting
    to be reading
    the same books
    and calculating
    the same numbers
    as yesterday.

(I reached fifth grade
but there's no money to buy
new books.
Mama uses the old books and
teaches me from her "fountain of knowledge"
    which means I do work I already finished
    and listen to her stories.)

Nothing ever changes
and nothing will ever change
because even getting the Jane Austen box set
is impossible.

Defiance

I say,
NO.

Today I want to ride
to the water park,
walk around,
see the trees,
fake lakes,
and statues.

Mama pauses,
takes a large breath
that makes her shoulders shudder.

Are you growing up on me?
Is this defiance?
she asks.

I don't know what it is,
but it feels good
for once
to set my hands on my hips,
tell her how things are going to be.

Mama's thin lips
pull so tight
against her tic-tac-toe teeth,
they disappear.

Let me put on my scarf,
she says after a pause,
and I'll come with you.

The Water Park

Blue sky today,
bursting trees:
    pink,
    white,
    tiny green new leaves.

We cross stone bridges,
listen to
old women
sing
in a chorus
of shrill,
wiggly
voices.

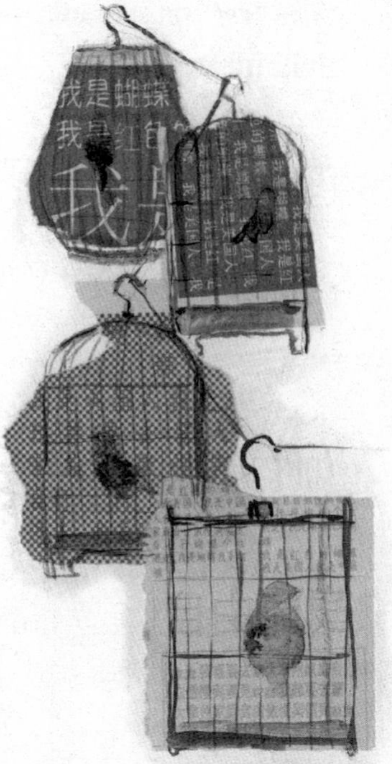

Listen to birds
in cages
suspended
from
tree branches
    (none
    as beautiful
    as my green Jim,

but boy,
can they sing!).

Watch a bout of
badminton
back and forth.

Shuttlecock
back and forth.

Everyone playing
is old and smiling.

The last time we were here,
Mama says,
was with Daddy
when you were a little girl.
You had a tricycle
and you rode it round and round
that flower bed.

She points,
laughs at the memory.

Mama takes off her long gloves
to let the spring sun warm her arms.
No one here
will care
who I am.

I wonder why
she thinks
anyone would care.

We are an old lady
and a girl
not drawing a bit of attention.

Leaving

We leave the gate,
the green-blue of park,
and step back
into gray city.

Mama looks back,
gaze lingering
on the lake,
the drooping willows.
She says,
We should do this again.

Her cheeks are pink,
even her faded freckles
stand out
like stars in a black night
but backward.

We should bring Jody here,
she says.

Which is not
what I was thinking
at all.

The Arrival

Late on Tuesday night
Jody lugs her big suitcases
(thump) (thump) (thump)
up the stairs.

There's no putting her back
because she's here now,
all of her.

Jody

She has short yellow hair
      like a boy,
a stomach
      spilling over
      the rim of her shorts,
and blue things
      that crawl up her legs

like worms
under pale skin.

Mama calls them
varicose veins.

I have them too,
she whispers.

She lifts her skirt,
shows me her leg skin,
all the bumpy
lines going up and down,
blue and green
like bruises.

I whisper,
I've never seen a Chinese person with those.

Mama says,
No, I guess not.

But I think
at least Mama
has the intelligence
to cover them up.

Gifts

Jody brings
tiny bits of chocolate
that arrive in their own
labeled bag
and are the shape of
fat teardrops.

Rich, soft
brown sugar,
not red,
not hard
like we have here.

Knitting wool
for Mama.

People magazine.

Mama's favorite
candy bar
with peanut butter
in the middle.
I get one too.

After that
Jody slaps her thighs.
That's all she wrote, folks.

I sit
cross-legged,
the chocolate bar
in my lap,
and let my hopes
wilt
like old flowers.

I wasn't expecting
Jane Austen.
After all,
it was impossible.

Impossible

Here,
Jody says later,
emerging from
my room,
where all her belongings
are piled on top
of a sagging
red
suitcase.
I almost forgot.
Dad sent these for you.

She hands me a box
with one end cut out

so books can slide in and out,
    Jane Austen books,
like it's no big deal,
like I haven't been dreaming
about this for months,
like Mama hadn't said
it was impossible,
a trouble,
a burden.

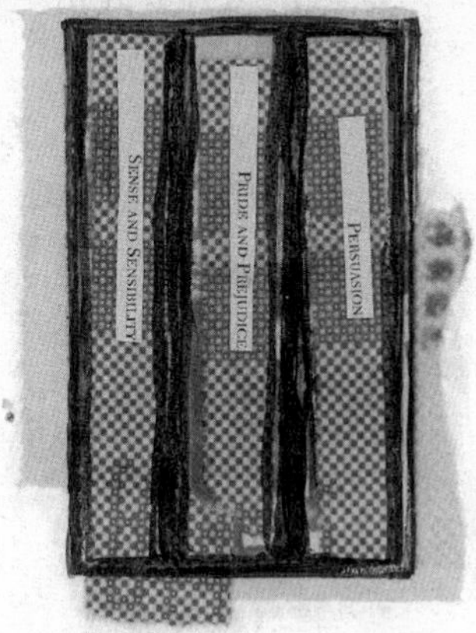

I peek at Mama to see if she's mad
at me for asking
when she said no,
but she's smiling
and her eyes gleam with tears
when she says,
Wasn't that nice of Daddy?

Jody Time

In the daylight
she sleeps in my bed,
her mouth open,
snoring.

At night,
when she should be asleep,
she's wide-awake
talking

LOUD-VOICED
to Mama,
who nods,
    yawns,
nods,
but collects
each Jody-word
like it's a
fleck of gold.

Holiday

Now that Jody's here
every day
is a holiday,
a drop-everything-and-be-happy
day,
a no-schedule day.

Jody says
crazy,
irrational things
like,
Let's take a taxi
to the American restaurant
for dinner.

A taxi!
To the American restaurant!

Mama takes special care
pinning back her hair,
sprays perfume,
and drapes her
    favorite scarf,
    covered in pink roses,
    around her neck
    and over her mouth,
pulls on
    newly washed
    white gloves
    up to her elbows
    and says,
        Let's go.

I stare at her.
Maybe Jody's presence makes Mama
forget about skin wrinkles
and outside air
and the long flight of stairs.

Mama catches my eye,
must spot my confusion, because
she pulls the rose scarf down
long enough to flash a smile.
    Just this once,
    she whispers.

One American Meal

No one stares here
because everyone
expects
foreigners
to arrive
at an American restaurant
in a taxi,
to sit at a table
covered in a red/white cloth,
to order plates
and plates
and plates
of food.

Mama,
away from the outside air,
in the restaurant cool,
unwinds her scarf,
pulls off her gloves,
    and smiles.

A waitress with many pins
stuck in her shirt
serves
heaps of lettuce
    covered in
    cold sauce,

meat in
    one big chunk,
    red in the middle,
onions cut
    into circles,
    fried all around.

The onions aren't bad,
but everything together
makes my stomach hurt.

At the end
Jody says,
My treat,
and puts a wad
of money
on the tray
for the waitress.

I can't help thinking
Mama and I
could survive
for one whole month
on the money
Jody just gave away
for one
American
meal.

Calling Willard

Two hours back,
then switch the
a.m. to p.m.,
the p.m. to a.m.

This is how you calculate
the difference
between Chinese time
and American.

Jody slaps her palm
to her forehead.
She's trying to figure out
when to call Willard
so she won't wake him up
at four o'clock in the morning.

Mama says,
Don't complicate it.
Fourteen hours behind in spring and summer,
fifteen hours in winter and fall.

Jody says,
That's not complicated, Ma?
If my phone would work
I could look it up.

And you need to buy an
international phone card,
Mama says.
Kara can take you.

Jody laughs.
Willard might have to wait to get his phone call
when I'm back on American soil.

Escape

There's only
snoring
or
LOUD
talking
or
Shush, you'll wake Jody
in our apartment now.

I run my finger over
the cover of *Pride and Prejudice*,
but don't open it

yet.

I've been waiting so long
it feels right to savor.

I try to draw
Zhao Bin
in my notebook—
capture
his smile
with the dimples.

When Mama
relaxes
on the couch,
her eyelids fluttering,
I make my escape,
leaving a note
on the table.

Gone for a bike ride
XOX

Meeting Zhao Bin

I wonder if he
can sense
I've been
drawing him,

because there he is
in the stairwell
when I'm coming up.
He stands at his gate
holding the handle

like he's not sure
whether to come or go.

I tuck my stubby hand
in my pocket,
my heart squeezing
too tight
to let my mouth
smile.

I say,
Hello.

Oops, wrong language.

Ni hao.

At the Top of the Stairs

At first I don't notice
Jody's loud talking
behind the front door,
because my heart is still soaring
from the Zhao Bin encounter.

It only hits me
when I touch the gate handle,
hits me

like staccato notes in music,
like machine-gun fire in movies.

I am still breathing hard
from pedaling
and stair-climbing
and smiling at Zhao Bin,
but I hear
Mama shushing Jody:
No no no no.

Jody shouts,
You act like she's the only one.
What about Dad
and my kids?
You've never even met my kids!
Do you know
how much
that hurts,
Mom?

Mama, quietly:
No no no.

Jody yells,
So this is it,
the way it'll be
for the next seven years?
You two

over here
just because
you were
born
stubborn?

Mama, whispering:
No no.

Jody screams,
What if someone
catches you?
What then?

Mama, firmly:
We've been fine
this long.
Don't talk about it.
Don't tempt fate.

Footsteps thump
across the floor.
A door slams.

I
tiptoe
back down
one stair
at a time,
sit

on the bottom
step
next to the
mailboxes
    rocking
until my heart
stops crashing,
    rocking
until I can see straight
enough
to stand up.

Guest

The restaurant lady,
with two bags
of white Styrofoam
containers,
passes me on the stairs,
glancing past me
with disinterested
eyes.

I follow
the hot, sweet smells
of chicken,
garlic beef,
and ginger
all the way to my door.

Jody pays
the restaurant lady
with cash
from our food envelope.

I find Mama hiding in her bedroom,
watching from the window
to make sure the delivery girl is gone.
Jody wanted outside food tonight.

My heart flexes
with resentment
even while my stomach growls.

I cross my arms,
take a breath to speak,
but Mama stops me.
Don't say anything, Kara.

I say it anyway.
We can't afford it.

Mama's jaw
tightens.
Mothers take care of
their children,
not the other way around.
I can pay for
one nice dinner.

I whisper,
After this
we'll be lucky
to afford cabbage!

Mama is usually
so soft and gentle,
but she has
a stiff pride.
There's nothing wrong
with rice for awhile
if we can make sure
our Jody
has a nice visit.

Her look tells me
the conversation
is over.

Yes

In the middle
of eating expensive food,
there's a knock
at the door
and I am the one to open it.

Zhao Bin is there,
standing

in the lighted
stairwell.

His mother grips both his shoulders,
speaks very slowly
in Chinese,
very slowly
because maybe she thinks
I won't understand.

Zhao Bin
must practice his English.
We hear
you are American.
Will you help him?

It is only me
facing them.

Mama hurried
to the back room
the moment
the knock sounded.

Jody chews
a large chunk of
pineapple chicken
and stares.

It is only me,
me and whatever I want to say,
whatever I want to do.

Yes,
I say in Chinese.
Yes,
I can teach him English.

It's the first time
anyone has asked me for something like this
and the first time
there wasn't a rule to stop me.

Mama Emerges

After I close the front door,
heart still pounding,
Mama's bedroom door creaks open.

Who was it?
she asks,
peeking out.

She must have been listening,
    but after all the years
        concealed in our apartment,
she has forgotten most of her Chinese.

Crossing a Line

Mama never gets angry,
    never yells,
    never blames.

But something snaps in her eyes
when I tell her
what Zhao Bin's mother
wanted
and
what I said.

What were you thinking?

Jody shrugs.
I would've stopped her
if I'd known what she was saying.

Mama scrapes the floor
as she yanks her chair back,
too angry
to speak.

Stomp

I wish there was a place to stomp to,
because Mama acting mad
makes me madder.

And all the madness
fizzling underneath comes
crashing out
like one of the trains
    roaring over the track,
    whistling,
    blaring,
    halting the bikes and cars
    for twenty minutes.

I wish there was a place to stomp to,
a door to slam,
but Jody's stuff is all over my room
and I'm sleeping with Mama.

Why don't you want me to have friends?
It isn't fair!

There's no place to go
but out,
so out I go,
leaving
all that delicious,
expensive
dinner
half-eaten.

Running

I've never done
anything
like this
before.

In my veins runs
fear
at what I'm becoming—
    a willful girl
    who leaves her mama behind
    because she's too angry to stay,

but also
excitement
and pride
at my Jane Eyre bravery.

I consider
Zhao Bin's
closed door
but keep going,
pausing to knock at
Zhang Laoshi's.

She always tells the truth
and I need to know
once and for all

why Mama
    holds me so close
    and why
    she hides.

Zhang Laoshi Explains

Of course
she has to hide,
Zhang Laoshi says,
tapping my forehead
with a gnarled finger
as if wondering if my brain is still inside.

Your mama can't /something/
because she's too old.

Besides,
you don't have /something/.

There they are,
the two /somethings/,
the /somethings/ that keep me
from understanding.

It's hopeless,
not even your older sister
could help.

If your mama left
she couldn't take you with her,
so she can't let them find her.

She's afraid
our neighbors
will report her.
She's even afraid
of me,
of what I could tell
the police.
You understand?

She sets a plate of
dried apricots
on the table,
round like gold coins.

The police?

She makes it sound
as if Mama
has done something
terrible.

But why . . . ?
I stop myself
because I won't ever understand
until I know

the meaning of
those two
    mysterious /somethings/.

Punishment

When I come home
Mama says,
Thank God,
and squeezes me long
    long
    long
    so long
it hurts.

Don't do that
to me
again,
you hear?

There's no forgiveness
in her release.

When she sends me
to bed early
I know it's
her way of telling me
never to let

my Jane Eyre bravery
push past her rules
again.

Mystery Words

I write the two mystery words
Zhang Laoshi said to me
in the back of
my textbook,
The Gift of Language,
    writing by
    the streetlamp light
    leaking through the crack
    between curtain panels.

Mama won't look
in my textbook.

Shou yang
Hu kou ben(r)

I don't know what they mean,
but when I go to Zhao Bin's house
to teach him English
I will ask.

I will teach
Zhao Bin English

whether Mama lets me
or not.

I just haven't told her yet.

Permission

I watch the clock,
measuring Mama's
silence,
knowing
she can't stay mad at me
for more than
one day.

She's knitting
with the soft wool
Jody brought.
Knitting
always makes her calm,
so I say,
Tomorrow's the day
I start teaching Zhao Bin,
using the same
certain
voice
I used
on our water park
day.

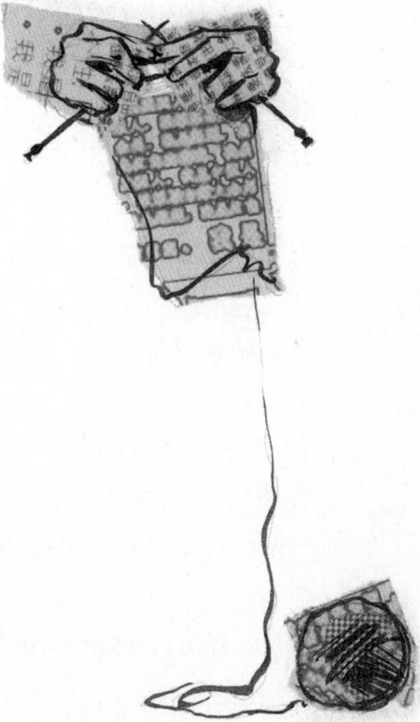

Mama's lips hum,
but she
keeps knitting.

He gets home from school
at six o'clock,
I say.

Mama drops the knitting in her lap
with a huff.
Okay,
you can go,
but I don't want
him in this house.
You can go to his
as long as his parents
are home.
But, please,
Kara,
no more of this.
It's a risk.

A risk of what?
I ask,
and immediately
hold my breath
waiting for her answer.

It's a risk getting attached,
Mama says

vaguely,
inspecting the intersection
of her needles.

So I ask,
Mama, why don't you like Chinese people?

Mama's eyes narrow.
I like all people,
Chinese and other kinds too.

I say,
But you never want to be around anyone
except Jody and me.

Across the room
Jody laughs
      or snorts
I can't be sure which.

Mama opens her mouth,
but no sound comes out.

She straightens.
It has nothing to do with
Chinese people,
Kara dear.
You are Chinese
and I love you.

I hesitate,
but I am growing braver.
Maybe it is Jody's
sharp eye
across the room
watching me,
possibly approving.
I thought I was American.

Mama nods.
You're both,
of course,
like we've always said.
You're both.

Jody speaks up
from the sofa,
where she is using a long white string
to clean between her teeth.

She's a big girl now, Ma,
growing out of your small life.
She should know the whole story.

For once
I like my sister, Jody.
For once
I don't mind her
butting in.
For once

I think she
understands
what it's like
to be me—
    a girl
    caught
    between two worlds
and my heart beats faster
because maybe Mama will tell me now
and nothing will be secret anymore.

But Mama shakes her head.
Not now, Jody.
You want to burden her with all that,
now,
when she's still a little girl?

I'm not so little,
I say.
You want me to stay little,
but I'm not.
I can take care of myself.

This is the problem with bravery:
it gets bigger and bigger
until words tumble out
that aren't quite right.

Mama shakes her head,
sets her lip,

stubborn,
just like Jody said she was.
You can help Zhao Bin,
but that's
it.

Independence

It doesn't matter
if Mama tells me
the truth.

I can find it out
for myself.

First Lesson

To Zhao Bin's first English lesson
I wear
my favorite lavender dress
with long sleeves
to hide my hand
even though the heat
makes beads of sweat
pop out on my forehead.

I brush my hair till it shines
and clip my lavender hair bow

in place,
dab on the vermilion lipstick
Mama never wears anymore.

Jody sees me
and whistles.
What kind of English lesson are you going to?

I don't answer.

I carry *Jane Eyre*,
the Jane Austen box set, and
The Gift of Language
down the stairs.

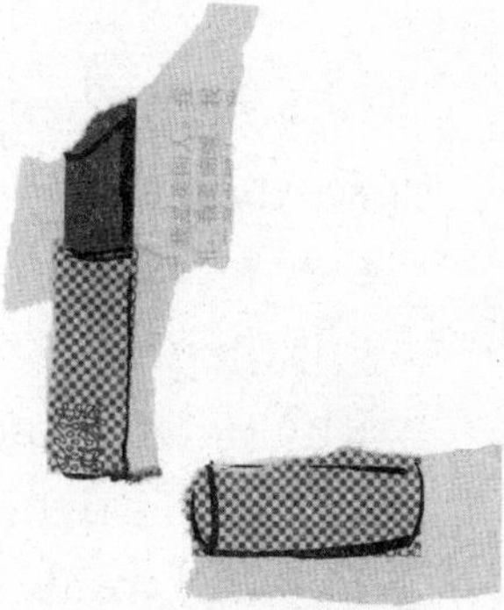

I'm
slightly sick,
shaky.
I hope I'm not
getting the flu.

I knock on the third-floor door,
listen to scuffling inside,
my heart pounding
like it's going to spring
out of my mouth.

All at once
they are all there,
smiling

offering me
    slippers,
    juice,
    cookies.

Their polished floor
looks new.

Smells of ginger
and furniture polish
linger in the cool,
filtered air.

The grandfather pulls out
a seat for me.
I take a cookie
from the plate
with my left hand,
keeping my right
concealed inside my sleeve,
    and smile.

Boring

Zhao Bin
looks at the pile
of books
I brought
and shakes his head.

Too difficult,
he says in Chinese.

The way he says it,
the way he avoids looking at me,
makes my stomach shrink.

His mother walks
through the living room.
SPEAK ENGLISH!

Zhao Bin
has soft,
embarrassed eyes.
The puckers are missing
from his mouth.

I'd like to bring them back
but my throat is dry,
my brain jumbled
with embarrassment.

Don't worry,
I say,
my voice a croak.
I'll help you.

Slowly
he pulls out
an English textbook.

It's boring,
he whispers in Chinese.

Boring,
I say in English.

Boring,
he repeats in English.

He's right—
it's boring,
so boring
I forget
to show him the secret words
written in the back of
The Gift of Language.

After an hour
I pack up my books
and Zhao Bin shuffles
to his bedroom
without saying good-bye.

Zhao Bin's mother yells,
SAY GOOD-BYE, ZHAO BIN!

From his room
he sighs.

That sigh withers
something
in my chest.

Maybe I'm the one
who is boring.

Thank You

Zhao Bin's mother
piles packages of food
into my arms:
    salted peanuts,
    dried apricots,
    fat cashews,
    a tin embossed with a picture
    of thin, white cookies.

Thank you, thank you!
she says in English,
    smiling,
    smiling,
then hurries me
out the door.

She would climb with me
all the way
to my apartment,

but I hold out my left hand
and assure her,
No, no, that's okay.
I can go by myself.

I can just imagine Mama's face
if I brought home company.

White Cookies

Jody's favorite
are the little white cookies.

You don't mind if I eat these,
do you?
she asks,
popping three at once
into her mouth.

Danish,
she mumbles,
turning the tin over.
I wonder if they sell these
in the States.

My Attributes

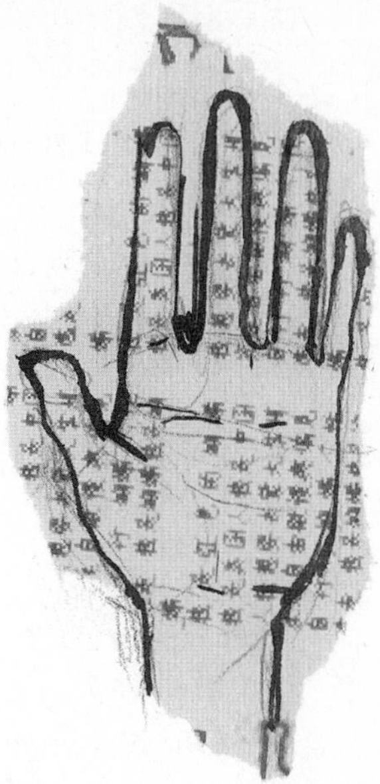

I list my attributes
on the fingers of my
left
hand
because *People*
magazine says
being confident
in yourself
makes you
more attractive
to the opposite sex.

1. I am eleven (pretty old, not a little
kid)
2. I am fluent in English (though my
Chinese needs improvement)
3. I guess I'm smart
4. I can ride my bicycle faster than
most people

Just the thumb left,
but I can't think of
another attribute.

Except
maybe,

it's silly but

5. I have long hair

Mama always says it's my glory.
I wonder if Zhao Bin thinks so too.

Clown

The next day
I only carry
The Gift of Language
even though
I know the two
secret words
by heart.

I still wear
vermilion lipstick
because *People* magazine says
red
never goes out of style.

Halfway
down the stairs
I rub the lipstick
off
with a tissue
because I start to think

confidence
has nothing to do
with lip color.

But then I put on more
in case
it does.

When he opens the door
Zhao Bin laughs.

You look like a—
he says in Chinese.

There's a word I don't know,
    a terrible, mystery word
    at the end of his sentence.

A what?

A—
He repeats
    the terrible, mystery word
and holds his stomach,
laughing.

SPEAK ENGLISH!
his mother bellows.

Zhao Bin keeps laughing.

He won't tell me in English,
he won't look it up
in his dictionary.

After two minutes
I excuse myself
to the bathroom
and find
the shadow of
old lipstick
blooming,
a rude,
red
halo
around my mouth.

Now the word
is no longer a mystery.

Tired

After one week
Jody is tired of China.

She lies on the sofa,
feet propped up,
the fan blowing
directly on
her blotchy face,

saying,
Investing in an air conditioner
wouldn't be a bad idea.

Mama says,
I'll look into that,
even though
I know she doesn't mean it.

I close my eyes and
dream of
Zhao Bin's cool,
nice-smelling
house.

Even when he laughs at me
and calls me a clown
it's better than here.

The First Line

I have not actually started
Pride and Prejudice.

I have read the first line
twenty-three times.

I am afraid to start,
afraid it will not live up to

my months of
expecting.

Instead of reading
I go back to the first page
and trace Mama's name
written in her old writing
over
and
over
with the tip
of my finger.

I wonder if she was
happy
when she wrote her name
with all those loops,
swirls,
and hearts over the *I*s.

Seeing her name written like that
is almost as good as a picture
of what Mama used to be
    before I knew her,
    before she knew Daddy,
    before she preferred to hide.

Dictionary

Zhao Bin has an electric
Chinese/English
dictionary
he uses
to figure out
what I'm saying.

I ask
if I can borrow it
a minute
and type in
the secret words.

Shou yang

/to adopt/

Hu kou ben(r)

/No Result, Please Try Again/

What is hu kou ben(r)?

Zhao Bin
mouths the word after me,
eyebrows crinkling.

My tones must be wrong.

But suddenly
he claps his hands,
rattles off something in Chinese
too fast to understand.

SPEAK ENGLISH!
comes the voice from the kitchen.

I'll show you,
he says.

He rushes
to the bedroom,
returns clutching a book.

Very important,
he says and
holds it out to me.

> A small book
> with rice-paper-thin
> pages:
> HOUSEHOLD REGISTER
> in English on the front.

When I reach for it he cries,
Don't touch!

SPEAK ENGLISH!
yells his mother.

Zhao Bin
ruffles the pages.
My grandmother here.
My grandfather there.
This is my mother.
This is my father.
This is me.

He jabs at the pages.
My eyes pick up
birth dates,
places of birth
before he slaps the book closed.

What happens if you don't have one of those?
I ask.

Zhao Bin shrugs,
chews his finger.
You're nobody.

He sets it
gingerly on the table
out of my reach,
and types frantically
on the electronic dictionary,
then flashes the screen at me.

/Identity/

Nobody

Awake
awake

All Zhang Laoshi's words
come together
with their missing puzzle pieces.

Awake
awake
in a bed
next to Mama
whose chest rises
and falls
so peacefully,
her white hair
a puff
across the
gray pillow.

I have no *hu kou*,
no /identity/

Shou yang
/to adopt/

The cold truth
washes over me, a vague
frozen shudder

that makes me roll
one side
to the other
    to the other
        to the other.

Mama and Daddy never adopted me.
I have no identity,
no mother,
no father,
no little red book
holding all my information
from the People's Republic of China.
Which means,
as far as the government is concerned,
I don't exist.

Replay

I replay the conversation
with Zhang Laoshi
in my head,
all the right words
snapped into place.

Your mama can't /adopt/
because she's too old.

Besides,
you don't have /an identity/.

It's hopeless,
not even your older sister
can help.

If your mama left
she couldn't take you with her,
so she can't let them find her.

She's afraid
our neighbors
will report her,
you understand?

Yes,
now I understand.

The Worst Part

Mama
has been
unhappy
because of me,
because of a decision
she made
long ago
to bring home a baby

she could never call her own,
to raise a child
who wasn't hers,
in a country
where she didn't belong.

She must regret it.

Headache

Mama has a headache today
    which keeps her in bed
        which means I'm stuck in this
            apartment box
                [living room]
                [kitchen]
                [bathroom]
                    with Jody
                        who never stops talking
                            who follows me around
                                talking
                                talking
                                talking.

I plan my escape
    into the sweaty
        summer air.

But Jody beats me to it.
Let's get out of here,
go on a walk or something,
let Mom get some sleep.

Nowhere is safe
and there is no excuse
I can think of
to get rid of her.

One Whole Walk

What do I talk to Jody about
for
one
whole
walk
when all my brain can think of
is the
truth
about
me?

It doesn't matter.
Jody talks enough for both of us.

I ignore the stares,
people pausing,
bikes slowing or
squealing to a halt.

They gape
at her
big white legs,
tallness,
paleness,
yellow-hairedness,
everybody wondering
why this
big white lady
is walking with this
small Chinese girl, talking
SO LOUDLY
in English.

Jody seems
not to notice.

McDonald's

Cool air
blasts
my sweaty skin,
almost
too cold.

Jody tells me she never
eats McDonald's,
but today
she'll make an exception
for me.

She orders
two Big Macs
two large fries
two large Cokes
two vanilla ice creams
swirled in cones.

I help her sift through
Chinese money,
pay the cashier
who giggles
behind her hand
and talks about *the fat foreigner*
when our backs are turned.

We sit at the window
in a place for two.

Jody eats
her whole Big Mac
and half of mine
(I don't like the sauce)
and shows me how to lick
my ice cream
to keep it from dripping.

The Coke bubbles
gurgle
inside my stomach.

Does Mama regret
bringing me home?
I ask the question out of nowhere.
Jody is midlick.

One of her eyebrows
rises
crookedly.

Hmm . . .
The noise is a grunt
and a consideration
all at once.

She sets her cone
on the table
without toppling it
and rubs her chin,
looking at me
like she's never
seen me before.

Good question . . .
Honestly?
I doubt she regrets
a single thing.

Mom wanted
another baby

more than
anything else
in the world,
but she could never have one
after me.

I think she's convinced
God reached down
from heaven
and placed you
in her arms
    and that's the plain truth
    since you seem to want it.

I set my cone
across from Jody's.
They sit
like two people
face-to-face.

It would have been better
if I'd never been born.

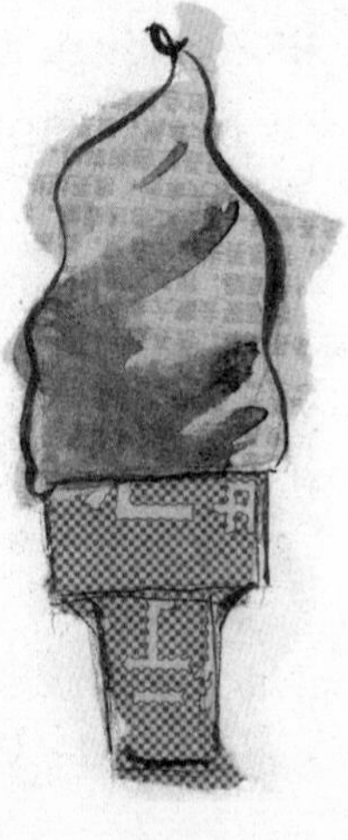

The words come out.
I don't know if I mean them,
but I want to see her reaction,
    want her to know
    how
    heavy

I feel, heavy enough
to cry.

I stare at the table
as Jody shifts, feel
the press of discomfort I've caused.

Hey now,
don't talk like that,
not after all Mom's done for you.
It's selfish.
She pushes herself to a stand.
Let's get going.

I'm selfish?
I'm not willing to be done
so I stay sitting.

I'm just saying . . .
Jody leans over.
You should be thankful.

I cover my face
unwilling to let her see
the wandering of my tears.
Thankful for what?
That I make everybody around me
miserable?

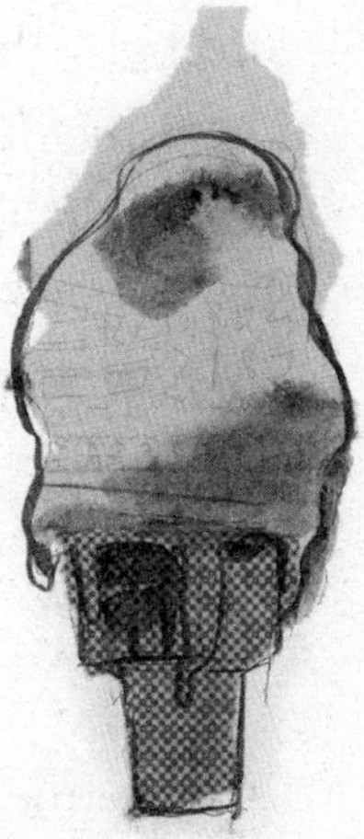

Come on.
Jody jostles my shoulder.

But I'm not done.
Maybe I should go away.
Then Mama can go back to Montana
and everybody'll be happy!

Jody presses me to her,
my face caught against the twin cushions
of her chest.
It's supposed to look like a hug
to all the people in the restaurant, but
to me it's a straitjacket.

I hold my breath
not wanting to smell
Jody's mix of
sweet sweat
and baby powder.
Don't you dare
talk like that.
Come on, Kara,
snap out of it, all right?
You wanna give me a heart attack?

No,
I don't want to hurt
anyone,
not even Jody,
especially not Mama.

I just want to stop
feeling bad
for all this
stuff I never knew happened
even though it all happened
    to me,
    around me,
    because of me.

I catch a glimpse of us
in the large wall mirror
as Jody guides me
to the door.
My face,
streaked with tears,
is shaded gray,
    a thousand years old.

Forgiven

Mama is up,
curled on the sofa
when we return,
clicking through
television channels.
    (Sometimes she likes to watch
    Qing dynasty soap operas
    that make her cry
    even though she can't understand
    the words.)

Her face
    brightens
    when she sees us
as if it's a television screen
suddenly
flipped on.

I hoped you were together,
she says.
Where did you go?
She leans forward
eagerly
as Jody says,
    McDonald's.
    We had a nice time.
    Kara got ice cream.

When Jody goes to the bathroom,
Mama cups my face
in her rough hands.
    Did you like that?
    Time with your big sister?

I nod a lie.
And just like that
I know
I've been forgiven.

The Question

I sit
across
from Zhao Bin
helping him
with verb tenses.

(I did not know
verbs
had tenses
because I always
tensed them
without
thinking.)

Studies/am studying/have studied/has been
studying
Was studying/had studied/had been studying
Will study/will be studying/will have studied/
will have been studying

Learning English is so much harder
than knowing it.

Then I realize
he's
staring.
At me.
I smile at the open page.

He smiles too,
dimpling.
Why do you
always
hide your arm
under the table?

His question strikes
like an invisible
icy patch
on the sidewalk
when I'm pedaling
extra fast:
    I tumble
    before I realize
    why.

Ways to Answer

Make up a story
about a
contagious
rash

or

Say I lost my
fingers

in a motorcycle
accident
and don't want him to see
because it's too gruesome

or

Slip my hand
from its
hiding spot,
lay my arm across the table
in full view,
and say,
I was born this way.

What I Say

American girls keep
their right hands hidden
at all times
except in the privacy
of their homes
when only their parents
are there.

In America
it's rude to ask
to see
a girl's right hand.

You need to learn more about American culture.

It's hard not to laugh
at Zhao Bin's
expression.

He glares down
at his verbs,
all the curiosity
knocked out of him.

Best to Hide

I keep
rehearsing
my conversation
with Zhao Bin.

My explanation worked,
so why do I dread
going back?

Why do I plan
to tell his mom
tomorrow,
I'm sick,
no more class
indefinitely?

I thought
he never noticed
anything different
about me,
never wondered
about my hand
or why a Chinese
girl was living
in an apartment
with an old American woman
nobody ever sees.

Maybe Mama was right,
    maybe it's best to hide,
    to stay safe,
so it won't hurt like his
every time
I make a friend.

Maybe safety and quiet,
schedule and thankfulness
are the most important things
in the world,
    like Mama said.

One Morning

At breakfast
I sip a bag of soy milk
through a straw.

Beautiful quiet
because Jody is sleeping.

She leaves tomorrow
early,
the clock ticks
hopefully.

Maybe after she goes
I can
finally read
Pride and Prejudice.

It will be wonderful
to fall back softly
into the old mold,
the one I wanted so badly,
for so long,
to break,
    but now
    yearn for
    like a warm sweater
    on a chilly day.

I'm almost glad
Jody came.
    Maybe
    she's not all bad.
    Just American.
Maybe
I won't mind her coming again
if her occasional visits
remind me
how much I love my life
alone
with Mama.

Fall

Jody appears in the doorway
at 9:10 a.m.
tipping slightly,
groggy with sleep.

But then she keeps tipping,
mumbling
as she
makes
one bursting
    fitful grab
    at a bookshelf
        where Mama's twelve glass animals nest.

A rush of
broken glass,
Mama's
high-pitched
shriek
that lingers
even as Jody's
body settles
lumpy
and still
across the living room
floor.

Help

I must have wings
because I fly down the steps
bang
on Zhao Bin's door
knock
knock
knock
until my knuckles split.

Oh, please come
please come
please come
please come
but no one comes.

Down one more flight,
leaping the last six steps.

Zhang Laoshi is already
waiting,
eyes burning
to find out what all the commotion is about,
her ears so sharp
she heard my sister fall
four floors up.

We Wait

Zhang Laoshi calls
the ambulance.

There is nothing to do
with my pounding
heart
    (ba-bum)
    (ba-bum)
    (ba-bum)
but climb the stairs,
wait with Mama,
who is on her knees
next to Jody,
who is breathing
in shallow
    fractured
gasps.

Mama
had the presence of mind
to sweep up the
glass animals.

I slide a pillow under Jody's head.

A tiny fear
chews at my brain
like a fat, black caterpillar—
that I caused this
somehow,
caused this stress
that led to sickness,
that all my bad thoughts
crawled,
crowded Jody,
all my wishing her away
made her sick,
made her fall,
made her not get back up.

I try to squish
that tiny black fear
between my fingers,
but it clings to life,
whispering,
    It's your fault if she dies.

Taking Jody

When they arrive,
our boxy apartment
becomes
    [boxier]
    [smaller]
    [crammed]
with pushing,
eager
people
and neighbors
gathered in the doorway.

I can't take
this mix of breath
reek of bodies
clamor of voices
feet
equipment
slamming
wedging
unraveling.

I push back
against a wall,
wait
with my hands
behind my back,

the nails of my left hand
digging into my right.

I want them to
take Jody,
make her better,
make this all go away.

I want her loud,
grating
voice to yell,
I'm fine, I'm fine,
as she pushes them back.

Jody's silence
scares me the most.

The Ambulance

The ambulance
is a low,
white van
with windows.

The security guards from our complex
mill around,
just as eager to hear
the news and
witness the chaos
as the neighbors.

Stern policemen arrive
with tucked-in blue shirts,
black boxes
blaring from their waists.

Mama stands still,
face blank,
eyes cloudy,
looking so old,
all of herself exposed
without her hat,
her scarf,
her long gloves.

When a policeman
asks for documents,
visa and passport,
she pushes him away,
stalks to the ambulance
and climbs inside
next to Jody
without a word.

I stand back in the shadows of the stairwell.
Invisible.

Decision

With a bang
the double doors
close.

Mama and Jody will be carried away
and I don't know where they're going.

Mama!
My voice is a baby bird's.
Mama!

She doesn't hear
from the white vacuum
inside.

I run at the van, pound
with full hand/half hand
together,
not caring who sees.

Mama!

She looks up,
her memory
snapping awake.

She points,
yelling English
as if that will make
the ambulance man
understand.

The man
who closed the doors
reluctantly
opens them again.
I climb inside.

Fear

As we drive away,
the stern policeman
who wanted Mama's documents

circulates
among our neighbors,
one eyebrow arched
in a rigid peak.

He watches
with a hawk's fierce eye
as our van rounds the corner.

I watch him
point after us,
    still talking,
    still asking,
and fear settles—
    dark
    deep
fear.

The Journey

Mama holds Jody's hand,
silent tears
running
snail-like
trails
down her
cheeks.

We sway
lurch
bump,
wait in long traffic
lines,
sirens
blaring.

The other cars don't budge.

The men in the van
wear stone faces.

Under the
clear breathing mask
Jody's skin
    is gray,
eyes sunken,
chest
    barely
    rising
and
    falling.

Diagnosis

The doctor
speaks English
and begins by telling us
she read at Oxford—
    whatever that means.

Her glasses are
        turquoise rectangles,
    her shoes
        gold flowers,
    her white hospital coat
        frayed,
        yellowing at the collar,
        gray at the cuff.

She speaks
    kindly,
nodding
    constantly,
her English a
    lilting song
over the hallway
    rush.

I strain to hear.

Pulmonary embolism.

The doctor's words are
distinct, but
I don't know what they mean.

Not a heart attack?
I ask.

No,
she says.
Blood clot in the lung.

Verdict

Two weeks
    in the hospital.
One month
    before Jody can
    take an airplane
    home
        to Matthew,
        Madison,
        big dog Sparky,
        and Willard.

One whole month
stretches
into the distance like forever.

Mama
and the doctor
pass words
back and forth,
a shuttlecock
of questions
and reassurances
lobbed
between them.

But she'll be all right?

She's out of danger.

She'll be all right?

Yes, she'll be all right.

That's the important thing.
She has children, you know,
back in America.
They depend on her.

I depend on you, Mama,
I want to say.
Because Mama has gone
from talking to no one
to talking to everyone
and I don't
feel
safe.

Go!

After the doctor leaves,
Mama grasps my shoulders.

I'll stay here at the hospital.
You go home,
she says.
Get the phone card
from my top drawer.
Call Willard
and Daddy.
Tell them what happened to Jody.
Then empty the envelopes
and bring the money to me.
Go!

I can't say it,
I can't say it,
because all Mama's hopes
ride high on me
obeying her now.

I cannot be
defiant
and break
her
heart.

But my soul screams
as I back
toward the
separating door:
    What if I lose you?

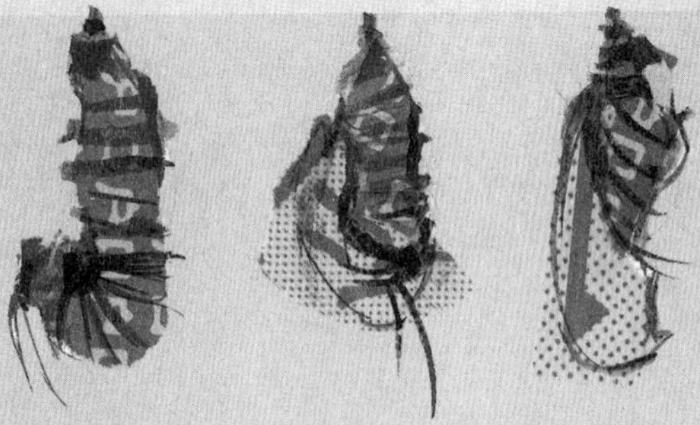

Part Two

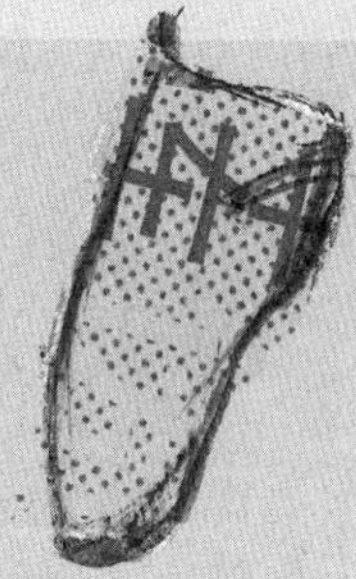

Dissolve

I Wish

My red bike is
locked outside
our apartment,
so I walk home,
sweat
trickling down
    my spine and
    the soft backs
    of my knees,
wish for even
a small breeze
to push me
on my way.

My shoes
beat
a rhythm
on dirty cement.

Still in my pajamas.

Mr. Wang

The gawkers are
gone,
except for one man
who stands

in the middle
of the floor
gazing at dusty footprints.

I pull back
against the creaking gate
and he turns:
    a tall man
    with a potbelly
    and bloodshot eyes.

You're the girl,
aren't you?
he says.
I am Mr. Wang,
the landlord.

My legs tremble
from fatigue
and fear,
but I cannot make them
move.

Come here.
He motions
with long
tapered
fingers
that draw me close
despite myself.
What happened?

I tell him
in my
halting
Chinese,
shuddering back
from the cigarette
stench
of his breath.

He says,
The police were here.
It's over now.
Go tell the old foreign woman
it's over.

The old foreign woman.
    He means Mama.

His palm slaps my shoulder
hard
as he casts a
significant glance
at my right hand
that I forgot to hide.

They'll find you a new place to live.
He looks sorry to say it.
    And the old foreign woman
    owes me a month's rent . . .
He flutters a hand.
    . . . at her convenience.

Stairwell

Blind
    with breathlessness
I don't see Zhang Laoshi
        until I plow into her.

Her thin body sways
    like a reed
        on the lake.

Sorry!
    I whisper,
        but even my soft voice
    fills the stairwell
        like a shout.

You're going? Where?
    she asks,
        clinging to the handle of her gate.

Mama and I
    both have to go,
I say.
    My verbs are all wrong,
    but for once, Zhang Laoshi
    doesn't scold.

She grips my arm,
but I can only see this is true
through eyes that
swim in
murky water.
I can barely feel her touch.

Zaijian,
she says.

It is a hopeful
thing to say.
"*Zaijian*" means "good-bye,"
but also "see you later."

Please

I don't want a new home.

I want
Mama.

Jody can stay
forever
if she wants
after she is well.

She can lie on our sofa
    and talk
    and talk
    and talk
as loudly as she likes.

I'm sorry I
complained,
    whoever heard me
        say I wasn't happy
    with my life
the way it was.

I'm sorry I
said all those
    words
to Jody
    to make her sick
        to make her fall
            to make her not get back up.

I'm sorry I didn't realize
I had
everything
when I had it.

Fly

Fly,
red bike, fly
    back to Mama
to the hospital
        before it's too late.

    Because maybe
the fat landlord is wrong,
    nothing is over.

We will escape
    to a different place,
a quiet corner of the world
        where /identity/
means nothing,
        where humanity
means everything.

Where
flimsy papers
that proclaim
you are somebody
don't exist.

Where family is
whoever you decide it should be
and all the questions
stop.

The Hospital

Jody's room
has a row of six beds,

laundry strung on a line across the window,

someone's panties flap,
a T-shirt drips a puddle.

The walls are half-blue/half-white
with shiny paint.

Fat silver radiators,
a funny smell,
half urine/half bleach.

Rice cookers
plugged in at the wall, spouting steam.

This is where Jody lies in a cold coma
on a flat white bed.

Moth

Mama is
a fragile moth
of night and shadow.

If I touch her
she might
flutter
away.

If I tell her
what the fat landlord said
she might
twirl
on pale wings
out the window
to Montana
        and forget me.

One Chair

There is only one chair
next to Jody's bed
so Mama
    pulls me into her lap,
    pushes her nose
    into my hair.

What happened?

I take a deep breath
and risk everything,
tell her everything
the landlord said.

Mama says,
I can't leave Jody.
If the police come
we'll work it out.
Did you call Daddy?

No,
I couldn't call
anybody.

I couldn't even retrieve
the phone card
or the money
because the landlord

blocked my path
to the bedroom door
and I didn't want him
to follow me,
to rob us.

When I tell Mama this, she nods,
pressing her fist
to her forehead.

Then she says,
Stay with Jody.
Hold her hand.
I'll go home to get the phone card
and the money.
I'll talk to Mr. Wang.

She hurries away
before I get a chance to say
good-bye
    or cling
    or cry
    or anything.

Holding Her Hand

Jody's hand
is cold,
freckled.

Her face behind the
oxygen mask
saggy.

A clock
suspended
in the hallway
flips through time
in red numbers.

I leave
just for a minute
every other
minute
to check
how long
Mama
has been
gone.

This time
it's up to
four hours
twenty-seven minutes
plus the thirteen seconds
counted in my head
on the slow walk back
to Jody's
bed.

What if she never comes?
What if she's been taken away?

Soup

The woman
watching over the girl
in the next bed
gives me
a bowl of soup.

After that,
she shares
    rice
    egg
    spare ribs
from a metal container.

I nod
my thanks.

She asks me questions
in Chinese,
pointing to Jody on the bed.

Where is this woman's family?
Why is she in China?
What's wrong with her?

I pretend not to understand.

Long Night

There is a crushing
    dark
in the ward
    when the lights go out.

All that's left is the
    rattle of curtain tracks
        as the nurses walk through,
    the bleep
        of machinery,
    a shallow cough,
    low groans
        from two beds away.

Jody's IV
    drips
    drips
    drips
but she does not wake.

Other patients'
relatives
care for them,
sleep in the hallway
on newspaper
spread out
on the floor
or across

two or three
plastic chairs
if they're lucky.

I sit straight,
    wondering if Jody will die,
    wondering if Mama will ever come back,
    hoping the frowning nurses
        won't force me to leave.

Waking Up

A nurse shakes my shoulder
and I wake
stiff and cold.

I fell asleep
bent forward,
my head
resting
on Jody's legs.

When I touch my face,
I feel the pattern of the blanket
embedded
in my cheek.

The nurse
eyes my

fingerless hand
as she says,
She's trying to speak.
Wake up
so you can listen.

Jody's oxygen mask
is gone,
her eyelids
flutter.

I lean close,
whispering her name,
gripping her hand,
which
isn't so cold now.

Jody's
eyes shift
under
lowered
lids.

Where's Ma?
asks her raspy voice.

I Don't Know

I don't know
is not an answer.
I can't make my mouth say it.
I cannot pass my tears,
my panic,
on to Jody
when she's sick.

She went to call Daddy,
I say,
which isn't a lie.
I just don't tell her how long she's been gone.

Instead of my panic
I give her my hope—
She'll be back soon.

Jody nods,
then
fades
to sleep,
to the rhythmic bleep
and drip
of her IV.

Questions

The woman
who takes care of
the girl
in the next bed
whispers,
eyes darting,
Where is the woman
who was here before,
the very old,
foreign woman
with the white hair?

At first
I pretend
not to understand.

But slowly
the persistence
of her questions
wears
through
my fear.

I don't know,
I whisper,
sniffing back a sob.

The woman nods.
Eat this.

She hands me *bing*—
flat bread
Mama told me is like a
tortilla
in America.

The woman tells me
the hospital staff
are asking questions.

They will move Jody
to the expensive ICU
if there is no one but a child
to take care of her.
The nurses are complaining
about the extra work.

I'm sorry,
she says.
I thought you should
know the truth.

I nod,
strangely
grateful
for her honesty.

I will take care of my sister
until my mother comes back.

Brave words
from a not-so-brave heart.

The woman tilts her head.
She does not ask me how Jody
could be my sister.
She only says,
Good girl.

Jody Wakes

Ma still not back?

I shake my head.

How long have I been asleep?
Worry darts behind her eyes.

Has anybody called Willard?
Does he know I'm sick?

I imagine
Willard,
Matthew and Madison,
and the big dog, Sparky,
all at home

eating American pizza,
expecting that
Jody is on her way
over the ocean.

I pat her arm
and say,
It'll be okay,
    even though every word
    could be a lie.

Even Jody

Jody can sit up
and drink soup
from the kind woman's supply.

I help her
with the spoon.

How long has she been gone?
Tell me,
Kara.

When I say
since yesterday afternoon
I'm queasy with
betrayal,

as if my holding
the words
unspoken
kept them from being
true.

Jody takes the news
quietly,
pale eyes
in a white moon face.
Where do you think she went?

She said she was going home,
I say.

I'll be fine,
Jody says.
Go home,
see if she's still there.

I protest
because the nurses expect
family
to take care of patients
and I'm already doing a bad job.

Let them earn their money,
Jody says,
the texture of her old
self

chafing
against her weakness.

But as I near the door
fear
    flutters
that
I will not find Jody
if they take her to the ICU,
that I will lose
absolutely
everything
I have called
mine.

Even the loud sister I never wanted.

Old Friend

At least
my red
bicycle is
waiting
where I left it
in the bike parking
area.

Hot tears
steal

down
my cheeks
at the sight of my old,
faithful
friend.

At least
I can still
fly.

At Home

Hands shake
inserting the key,
fingers slippery
with sweat.

Click on the lights.

Dusty floor
from dirty shoes
traipsing through.

Most of the furniture gone:
    the couch,
    the TV,
    the dining room table.

Mama's wardrobe burst open,
clothes scattered,
a missing suitcase.

A letter
scrawled in Mama's
sideways
writing:

Must go with police.

Daddy on his way.

Don't be alarmed—
the landlord
took furniture
in exchange
for rent.

I don't know
what will happen,
Kara dear.

I failed you.

Remember this:
I love you
more
than

words
can
say.
Always have and
always will.

Maybe

Maybe
Daddy will come
and save us.

Maybe
he will buy me
a sugared hawberry stick
from a street vendor,
pay the landlord
the money we owe,
and get back all our furniture,
    even the birdcage.
        Hey there, Jim,
        good Jim,
        there you go, Jimmy.

Maybe
he'll bring Jody back
to our apartment,
then announce,
Teaching English is my thing,

China's my thing,
my family's my thing.
Who needs Montana
and mountains
when I can have my girls?

Maybe
he'll bring back Mama's smile,
make us a family again.

Maybe
it's just like the Jane Austen box set:
    seems impossible
        but then
            there it is.

Backpack

Three pairs of underwear
Two shirts
One pair of shorts
Two toothbrushes
One tube of toothpaste
Jody's fancy American facial wash
Ten bags of strawberry yogurt
    with straws
One loaf of bread
One jar two-thirds full of peanut butter
One plastic knife

Jane Austen box set
and, of course,
Jane Eyre

I leave a note for Daddy
beside Mama's,
a page ripped from my
school notebook.

I tell him which hospital,
    what to say to a taxi driver,
    which floor,
    which room,
and leave the door ajar.

Handshake

A shadow waits
at the base of the stairs
next to the rows of metal mailboxes.

When Zhao Bin emerges
my instinct is to
run,
but he has already seen me.

He holds out his hand.

Good luck,
he says in English.
Perfectly.

I stuff my stub hand
in my pocket, grasp
his extended hand
with my whole one.

    Up, down,
    up, down
go our hands
in a strange
imbalanced
swing
until they slip apart.

He holds the metal security gate
open
so I can step out
into the night,
run,
face burning,
to my bike,
wishing I had the courage
to tell the truth,
to hold out my half hand,
to say a real good-bye

to an
underestimated
friend.

Dark Ride

My bicycle wheels spin
down the dim road.

The cars'
headlights stream light
but several
streetlamps have
burned out.

A man
calls out from the shadows,
but he's no one I know.

I pedal faster.

This is a poor part of town
with black alleys.
A tattered, upside-down
luck sign flutters in a
patched doorway.

A woman stares out a window,
the room behind her
lit in red.

Still There

Jody is
in the same bed,
    same ward,
not sleeping,
her eyes like an owl's
in the dark.

I tell her about Mama,
that Daddy is coming.

I ask her
if she thinks
they'll put Mama in jail
because she didn't turn me in
when she found me.
Maybe if we told the stern policeman
that Mama didn't mean any harm
taking me in,
that I like living with her,
maybe he'd understand.

Jody's brow crinkles,
a weak
interrupted
series
of furrows.

You think Mom's in trouble
because of you?
she says.
Oh, honey,
Mom hasn't had a visa
to live in China
since Dad lost his teaching job.
I'm so sorry,
Kara.
I should've told you.

Clear

Now so clear,
all the hiding
and whispering
and bundling up
to go
outside
so a foreign woman
wouldn't be recognized,
wouldn't be asked
for her paperwork.

Big love,
stupid love,
just like Zhang Laoshi said.

Questions

What will happen to Mama?
Will they put her in jail?

Jody thinks
they'll repatriate her,
which means
they'll send her back
to her Montana mountains.

That doesn't sound so bad
for her.

Imagine

I imagine
Mama
getting back to her mountains,
    to her husband,
    her grandchildren.

I imagine her
smiling
all the time
the way she smiled
in that picture from Hangzhou,
the way her name smiles
because she wrote it
with curls and hearts.

I imagine all of them
without me.

I imagine myself
forgotten.

Attributes

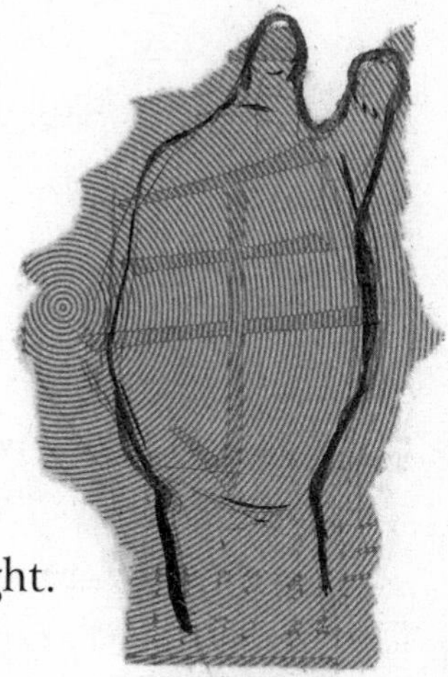

I should have counted
my attributes
on my other hand,
the hand with only two nubs.

That would have been about right.

Soft-Voiced Jody

Jody's voice
has gone soft,
squishy,
different.

For the first time
I can see her
as the mother
of two children who are
just a little younger than me.

Don't give up yet.
We'll figure something out,
okay?
We're not going to leave you here
alone,
you hear me?

I want to believe her.

Smoke

I don't know what happens
to an almost-twelve-year-old girl
with bad Chinese,
with only two short fingers
on her right hand.

I don't know what happens
to a girl who's
been raised to be
American,
but who isn't really
American
at all.

I don't know what happens
to a girl
with no /identity/
no /adoption/
no real family.

Maybe Daddy will stay for a while
until they get this thing
with Mama's visa
sorted out,
Jody says,
but her words
are thin as smoke,
carried
away
as soon as she speaks them.

Daddy

Three days
waiting
in one room,

then
waiting is
suddenly
unexpectedly
over.

Daddy arrives
(with Willard)
and I see
him as if
for the first time:
a bald man
with thin arms

who squints
through thick glasses.

This is my father,
the savior,
a very old man.

I push my face
into his chest,
wrap my arms
around his body,
nod when he says,
You've grown
        as if he's surprised.
All the while I
attempt to latch on
to a rush of relief
        that never surfaces.

Translator

I'm Willard's translator.

He wants Jody
        moved to a private room,
        money is no object.

Then he changes his mind.

He wants her
    transferred to Beijing
    to the international hospital,
    pronto.

He waves insurance cards
    that mean nothing here.

The administrators
begin to mutter,
to say,
Pay us up front,
which means
right now.

Willard says
that's not how it works in America.

The administrators want cash,
but all Willard waves in their faces
are plastic credit cards.

Negotiator

Daddy
hangs at the edge
of the ward
near the door
only coming close

to hug
Jody
and
me,
tapping his foot
all the time,
a cell phone
attached to his ear.

He's talking to
the American Embassy.

Those police better treat her right
or heads are gonna roll,
I hear him say
in a voice too loud for the ward.

Everyone else has gone silent.

Taken

Four
policemen crowd
the room
followed by administrators
brandishing pens
and clipboards.

Four
in China
is an unlucky number.
“Four”
in Chinese
has the same sound
as “death.”

Just different tones.

Four
policemen:
two for Daddy
to take him to Mama,
two for me
to take me away
somewhere else.

A policewoman lays a slender hand
on my shoulder.

Where are they taking her?
Jody asks.

All the women in the ward
stare at me
like I'm a finally captured
criminal
living under
their noses.

Their faces whirl,
    blaming
    blurring
    blinding.

Who can save me?
    Daddy?
    Jody?
    Willard?
But they hold still.

No one moves
even a notch
as I'm guided to the
door.

Behind me,
Jody begins a
LONG
HIGH
wail.

Nurses shush her,
scolding the police,
the administration,
for causing commotion.

The room is packed
with people
watching,
elbowing.

We'll find you,
Daddy calls
after me.
They won't get away with this.

Who are *they*?
The police?
The law?

The policewoman
pushes me
ahead of her through
the crowd.

Jody's wail
follows us to the elevator

and the door slides shut.

New Place

I slump in the back
of the police car
alone
listening to the two officers
discuss me
through the glass divider.

This is
Er Tong Fu Li Yuan,
says the woman
as we drive past
the guardhouse
through a silver gate
that folds back
like a hand fan.

I only recognize two words:
"children"
"garden"

I wish I could feel
something
to remind me
I'm alive,
but the only ache
remaining is a repeated memory:
the moment
when Daddy should have moved

to reach for me, but
didn't.

It's all
a slow-moving dream
as the gate creaks
shut
behind us
and I am
locked
in.

Miss Li

Miss Li
works in the office
on the second floor.

She is pretty
and young
and wears
tight pants
with high heels.

I sit in a wooden chair
waiting,
thinking
something is missing.
My foggy brain
can't remember what.

There is a printer
and three computers
in this room.

The desk
at my elbow
has photos under the glass
of smiling babies,
all of them
with foreign parents.

Miss Li
nods at the pictures.
We'll find you a new family
very soon,
she says in Chinese.

I already have a family,
I say.

Miss Li laughs
like I've made a joke
and goes back to
            tap
            tap
            tapping
her keyboard.

I just remembered
what I forgot.

My heart turns hard as stone.
My backpack
at the hospital.

I have come here
empty-handed.

Chinese Name

I curl and uncurl my fingers
around my right hand.

Do you have a Chinese name?
Miss Li asks.

I shake my head.

Do you have an English name?

I nod.

You are fluent in English?

Again I nod.

Miss Li's eyes widen.
You will be easy to match.

She pats my head,
writes quickly on a
pad of paper,
swift Chinese characters,
flowing and swaying.

This is your new name.
A gift for you.

I take the paper
although I can't read
Chinese.

My Room

Miss Li takes me
down a long hallway
and up two flights of stairs
into a big room
with fluorescent lights
and red-and-blue squishy mats
tiling the floor.

We stand in the doorway.
Miss Li removes her heels.
I bend down
to untie my sneakers.

There are lots of kids here,
big kids,

and two older women who must be helpers
because they wear blue aprons
over their clothes.

In Chinese they are called
ayis—
"auntie" in English.

The two *ayis* stare at me
and throw out comments
to one another
across the room.

I can't understand everything,
but I understand this:

I thought she was a foreigner.

No, she's a Chinese girl.

I want to answer
the way Mama
always answered.
I'm both.

But Miss Li cuts in.
She is Chinese,
raised by foreigners,
so her Chinese is bad.

The *ayis* laugh at that.

I speak a little,
I say
then wish I'd kept my mouth shut
because they exchange
amused glances.
Even the kids
sitting at a big table
look back and forth at each other
like I'm a joke.

I don't know where I am.

I don't want to stand in the
doorway of this room
and let everyone stare at me.

Where do I go?
I whisper to Miss Li.

There are kids everywhere,
but they all seem to have problems—
    they sit in wheelchairs
    or lie on the floor mats,
    their bodies twisted.

The room is filled
with the sound of funny breathing
and the faint murmur

of tinkling music
from a small CD player
plugged into the wall.

There are whispers, too,
always whispers
from the kids who sit
around the table.
One girl taps her pencil
in time to the music
while she watches me.

This is your room,
Miss Li says.
You sleep here
and study here
and go to the cafeteria
for meals.

I don't see any beds,
only brightly colored floor mats.

Everyone watches
and I begin to wonder
if they're waiting for me to cry.

What's wrong with you?
one of the *ayi*s asks,
a wide-shouldered woman
with large curls sprayed stiff.

Her way of speaking slowly
reminds me of Zhao Bin's mother.

I don't know what she means,
so I say,
Nothing.

Miss Li holds up my arm
and tugs back the sleeve
to reveal my
stub
hand.

Then she explains
my difference
to the *ayis*
using technical words.
    All I recognize is
        shou
            shou
                shou
                the Chinese word for "hand."
The *ayis*
nod
and say, *Ah, ah, ah.*

Miss Li releases my arm.
No problem,
she says in English.
    The kindness in her smile
    takes me by surprise.

Looking Around

There are three other kids
in my room
who can walk besides me.

One wears braces on his legs
and staggers,
another is a gentle girl
with a round face
and constant smile,
who traces
simple characters
on paper
over and over,
but doesn't speak.

There is also a boy
who howls,
breaks pencils,
throws himself
on the floor
until one of the *ayis*
agrees to take him outside
to play.

And there is me,
taking all this in
      all this in
      all this in.

Beds

It's not yet dark
when the *ayis*
pull out fifteen beds
stacked five high
against the wall.

We have enough,
the *ayi* with the stiff curls
says.
Don't worry,
you'll sleep here.

I wasn't worried about sleeping mats,
I was worried about sleeping
in this one room
with all these other kids,
even boys,
and all the noises.

The beds are small frames
low to the ground
with thin mattresses
covered in scratchy sheets.

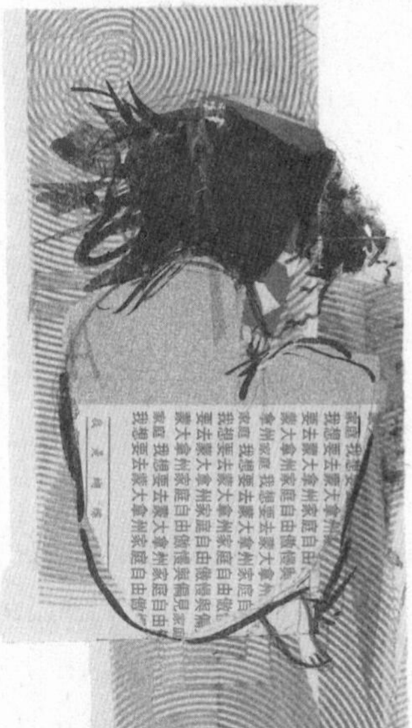

The pillow slumps
hard and flat.

I sleep in my clothes.

The Same

I spend the morning
sitting at the table
with the kids who are
in wheelchairs
and the boy in leg braces.

The quiet girl with the round face
is also here,
and,
when he's in the mood,
the boy who breaks pencils.

They all work,
writing characters
in thin books with
transparent
pages.

My hands
twist in my lap.
I don't have a book
or a pencil
and I'm too afraid
to ask
if this is something
I'm required to do too.

The kids who lie on the mats
have problems either with their brains
or with their bodies so severe
the *ayi*s don't try to sit them at the table.

The kids at the table don't speak to me,
    though they speak to the *ayi*s
    and one another
    just fine.

One of the *ayi*s hands me a pencil
and a blank sheet of white paper.
She gives me no instructions,
so I draw Mama's face.

Everyone must be watching
my tears drip, smearing
the gray pencil marks.
I cry stubbornly
refusing to look away
from Mama's face
or up
at any of them.

This afternoon the foreigner comes,
one of the *ayi*s says.
She might be talking to me.
None of the other kids respond.

I don't know

who the foreigner could be,
so my stupid heart thumps hope:
    maybe Daddy,
    maybe Willard,
    coming to take me away?

The Foreigner

The foreigner is
a man,
    not Daddy,
    not Willard,
but I am too weary
from the energy it took
to hope all day
to be disappointed.

He speaks English
and tells me his name is Toby.
He comes here
every afternoon.

He is short for a foreigner,
just a little taller than me
even though
he's twenty-six years old.

He's from
New Zealand,
but I don't know what that means.

He talks a little funny,
but I can understand him
all right.

I'm a physical therapist,
he tells me,
squatting next to my chair.
I help with the CP kids in this room,
make sure they're getting their exercise.

I like his voice,
the smoothness of it.

"CP" stands for
"cerebral palsy,"
he tells me,
children who walk with a stagger
and a jolt
or not at all,
who need help eating,
whose brains
were hurt somehow
before they were born
so they can't move
like they want to.

Toby helps them learn
to sit,
walk,
feed themselves.

Toby speaks Chinese
better than me
even though he has
    seaweed-colored eyes,
    curly brown hair,
    and skin lighter than Mama's.

My New Name

Toby reads the name
Miss Li gave me,
the one she wrote
on the slip of paper.

Liu Xiao Ling

Nice name,
means tinkling jade.
It suits you.

I shake my head.
Am I green?
Do I tinkle?
How does that suit me?

Toby laughs.

I meant to be snotty,
not funny,
but Toby says,
Hilarious kid,
and ruffles my hair.

Translation

Toby tells me everything that's happening,
all the things he learned about me
from Miss Li,
while he stretches a boy's
curled feet
forward and back.
Since you're an older child
Miss Li will put you on a list
to have you adopted quickly
to an English-speaking country.

Like Montana?
I ask.

Toby says,
Is that part of America?

It's where my mama and daddy live,
I say.

My daddy's
coming to get me
to take me there.
He said he'd find me.

Toby pauses.
I'm not sure.

He's not looking at me.
I know
I've said something wrong, maybe
    too hopeful?

I blurt out
about my backpack
with *Jane Eyre*
and the Jane Austen box set
left at the hospital.

Toby says,
That's a shame,
and wags his head.

My eyes prickle,
because it's more than a shame.
Those things,
    from my toothbrush
    to the books with Mama's
    curled writing inside,
were all I had left
to call my own.

Even today's clothes came out of a bin
labeled with my size,
    the character for "medium."
I don't know what happened to the ones
I wore here.

I push down the wish
I shouldn't make—
    that I'll get my stuff back
    somehow,
    some way.
That unreasonable hope buoys
like an empty plastic bottle
floating on water.

    But why do I bother hoping
when hoping never works?

Pretending

I lie flat on my back
during rest time.
    I haven't had rest time
    without books
    since I was three, probably.

My heart keeps me awake.
    (ba-bum)
    (ba-bum)
    (ba-bum)

If I close my eyes,
plug one ear with my finger,
and the other ear with the pillow
to block out the bellows of the boy who breaks pencils,
I can pretend I'm home
in my old bed
in my old room
before Jody
    before sickness
    before policemen
    before the world cracked open
    and took Mama away.

Evening

We eat dinner
as a group
in the cafeteria,
except for the kids
who are difficult to move.

Cabbage,
chunks of meat,
and rice
served on a silver tray.
Soup from a huge pot,
thin like water,
in metal bowls.

Toby arrives
just as I'm helping to stack the trays
at the end.

Thought you might need this,
he says
and winks at me.

There,
hanging from his hooked finger,
is my backpack.

I grab hold of it,
clutch it to my chest.
Thank you!

I met your sister,
Toby continues.
She'll come visit
as soon as she's discharged.

"Come visit"
doesn't sound much like
taking me away.

But if a backpack can appear
when I least expect it,
maybe a miracle can happen too.

Tired

I should be tired,
but every time
I drift asleep
I'm falling
    falling
    falling.

I wake
with a jolt,
this new place
seeping again
into consciousness.

The smell here is similar to the hospital:
    sickness,
    medicine,
    porridge,
    disinfectant,
    pee.
But the sounds are different,
everything closer,
more compacted:
    the gurgles,
    soft snufflings
    without the bleep
    of machinery,
    a snore,

the far-away wail
of a baby
perhaps recently left
outside the silver gate,
still crying for its mama.

No relatives gather.
This is the home of lonely children.

Holding Pattern

Three more days
of sitting
while the kids at the table
learn.
Three days of drawing
everything from my memory
on loose pieces of paper
that fill the spaces in my backpack.

It's worse than
the schedule at home,
so much worse,
because there is no red bicycle,
no errands to run,
nowhere to be
but here.
And worse,
no Mama.

I chafe,
then
make up my mind to ask.
Pointing to the thin paper
the others use, I say,
Can I do that, too?

The *ayis* whisper together,
then ask Toby,
who shrugs and says,
Can't hurt.
But that's not enough
for them.
They must get Miss Li's approval too.
She strides in
wearing bright,
beautiful
turquoise pants.
She explains
through Toby

that there's no point
doing the table work with the others
because
I'll be leaving soon.

Adopted,
she says in Chinese,
the word that used to be
a mystery.

She lays out the facts:

> *It would be too difficult*
> *to catch up*
> *in the Chinese school system.*
>
> *You can't read*
> *or write*
> *Chinese characters.*
>
> *Might as well wait*
> *to start school in America or Canada*
> *since that's where*
> *you'll be going.*

I say,
What am I supposed to do
all day?

Toby says
he could use some help
with the CP kids
if I'm so inclined.

But I'm not
so inclined.

How can I
help anyone
when
I can't even
help
myself?

Visit

Jody and Willard
sit in the director's office
side by side
like clay statues.

Jody's voice is soft,
still not Jody's.

I'm sorry,
so sorry.

Mom and Dad
weren't allowed to say good-bye.

The officials were angry
Mom stayed so long without a visa.
They were also angry
that Dad helped her.

He'd been bribing everyone
for years
so Mom could stay.

It's all my fault.
If I hadn't gotten sick,
if I'd never come to visit . . .

Willard says,
Now, now,
it's nobody's fault.
Everything was bound to fall apart eventually,
and he gives me a look that tells me
I should agree with him
to make Jody feel better.

I don't know
if I agree
with anybody,
though I hate
to see Jody,

    booming
    loud
    Jody,
quiet
shriveled
crying.

Rain dashes
the window glass.
I imagine Mama
flying away
through this drizzling sky
toward her mountains
without me.

Was she sad to go . . .
    or relieved?

I turn that
bitter
question
    over
    and
    over,
a sour lozenge
on my tongue.

The rain quickens,
rattling the pane.

Are you getting enough to eat?
Jody asks.
You look thinner.
Are you brushing your hair?

Maybe you could take me,
I whisper.
Now that I have the paperwork
and an official name.
I mean,
if Mama and Daddy
are in too much trouble . . .

The look that passes between
Jody and Willard
tells me
I've said something wrong
    again.

I don't think that's possible,
sweetie,
says Jody.

The word "sweetie"
doesn't sound right
coming from Jody's
mouth.

I nod,
    silent
empty,
stare at my hands
until they
leave.

Better that way.

Lost

I almost wish
they hadn't come
because at least
when I thought
Daddy was still in China
I had hope.

Three Weeks Later

Toby tells me
my picture is on a website
showing older children
who need homes.

Your paperwork is done.
Now we wait for a match.
It won't be long.

But
I don't want
any family
except my own.

Possibilities

What about Jody?
Could she adopt me
and let me live
with Mama?

I'm desperate enough
to ask,
to push away
the memory of the doubtful,
sorry
look
between Jody and Willard
in the director's office,
the look that said they
wouldn't want me
even for a temporary daughter.

Toby sighs.
There are lots of restrictions.
They might be the right age,
but there are other
factors—

the Chinese government requires
healthy bodies, for one thing,
and a certain amount of money
in the bank.
I'm not sure . . .

He trails off.

I suck in a breath,
try again.

But if I go to America
with a different family,
will they let me visit
Mama and Daddy
in Montana?

Toby shrugs.
It's possible.

A small hope
struggles in my chest
    that my new parents will understand,
    that they'll take me over the mountains
        to Montana,
    that maybe, just maybe,
    they'll let me live with Mama and Daddy
    once they realize
Mama and Daddy are my true family.

What if I want to live with
Mama and Daddy?
Do you think they'd let me do that?
I ask.

Toby scrambles the long bangs
that hang in my eyes.
Your new family will want you, silly goose.
They won't come all this way to give you up.

I'm not a silly goose.
And I don't want him to be right.

The Lucky One

I wonder about the other kids
in my room—
    when they'll be adopted.
If new families want children so badly
    why can't they pick one of them
        instead
and let me go back to Mama?

There isn't an answer for everything,
    at least
not a good one.

Toby says most of the kids in my room
won't get adopted,
    their needs are too big.

My needs are smaller.

He says
    I'm the lucky one.

The way most of the kids
ignore me,
they must think
I'm lucky too.

    Too lucky to be a friend.

From Mama

Toby calls me
out of the room
and gives me
a package
from America,
from Montana,
for me.

We move away from the other kids
    to an empty office with a world map
    pinned to the wall.

I'm grateful
    because those other kids
    already don't like
that I have a backpack full of stuff
from my old life.
They don't say so,
    but I know it
from the way they watch me,
pretending not to watch me.

Mama sent me
a pair of wool socks
for the cold days,
ChapStick,
lotion that smells like
white flowers,
her favorite candy bar.

Toby calls the box
my American care package.

I treasure Mama's note most,
brush the paper
to my lips
to catch any scent
that might linger.
I imagine her writing
all these words.

Kara, we've contacted our congressman.
We're going to try to bring you to Montana
to live with us,
to be our daughter
once and for all.

My heart swells
as big as the blow-up ball
Toby sometimes bounces
between the kids on the floor.
My chest aches
with wondering.
Maybe it's not wrong to hope?

Coat

Toby brings me a green
puffy coat,
an early Christmas present
from the foreign volunteer group
that sponsors the orphanage.

There will be a show,
he tells me.
Will you sing a Christmas song
in English?
The volunteers would be delighted.

I accept the green coat
two sizes too big
because it's getting cold outside
    and inside, too
    and no one has brought blankets
    for us to sleep under.

I tell him I will sing
"Away in a Manger"
because Mama played it
every Christmas
and taught me to sing along.

Even after
we sold our electric piano,
Mama's fingers tripped
over the table edge,
her voice pale
as breath mist
in cold winter air
singing about that baby,
no crib for a bed.

There are lots of babies here,
maybe worse off even than baby Jesus.
        I'll sing it for them.

The Other Family

An envelope arrives,
this time from Florida,
another place in America.

The letter is all in exclamation points:

We're the Gurnsey family!
From Tampa!
We're so excited to meet you!
To bring you home!
To be our daughter!
Forever!

There are six of us!
But room for one more!

Love,
Your forever family

They include a picture:
    two brown-haired parents
    two blond-haired older boys
    two black-haired girls
        kind of like me
        but with two full hands each.
They all look so smiley
    I can see all their teeth,

and they wear jeans
    and shirts with checks:
        orange for the girls
        blue for the boys.

I stuff the letter and photo in the envelope,
slip it in the front pocket of my backpack
so the other kids don't see.
    I'm betraying Mama
    just touching it.

Dilemma

After the new letter
I wait for Toby
to ask his opinion
about this new family
of smiley people
who use words like
"forever"
when they talk about me.

But Toby doesn't come.
He's on a trip in
Southern China,
    Miss Li says
    when I sneak
    to the office
    to ask.

I try not to let hurt
dig a hole
of resentment
because he didn't tell me
he was going.

Helping

Back from the office,
I pause in the doorway
to watch one *ayi*
haul the CP boy
Xiao Bo
from one side of the mat
to the other.

Aiya!
she exclaims,
wiping her forehead
on a thin towel
slung over her shoulder.

Xiao Bo
tips.
She lurches to catch him,
rolls him on his stomach,
where he curls
in a crooked ball.

She is old,
not as old as Mama,
but too old
to stoop
and carry
and drag
a big boy
like Xiao Bo.

Ayi,
I say
from the doorway.
Wo bang bang ni—
I'll help you.

Her tense face
slides
into relief.
Xie xie,
she says.
Thank you.

Nervous

How do I play
with a kid
who can't move?

I try to remember
things Toby did.

I drag over
a special chair
for him
to sit in.

The *ayi* helps me
strap him into it.

Here,
she says,
handing me a bowl
filled with white
mush.
It's time for him
to eat.

I've never fed
anyone
except myself.

But we manage,
one spoonful
at a time.

Laugh

This boy,
Xiao Bo,
has a sense of humor.

When I miss his mouth
and porridge drips off his chin,
he actually laughs.

Person

They may look
too difficult
to love.

This boy
whose crooked
body
won't obey.

This girl
with her lopsided
smile,

hands held
stiffly at her chest.

But after days of this,
when I
sit behind
Xiao Bo,
he rocks back,
        smelling
        the same as I do—
        like the orphanage
                but mostly like a person
                with a little hope
                mixed in.

And when his Velcro-short hair brushes
my cheek,
we are two friends
sitting together
on a mat
in the rare autumn sunshine.

Photos

Toby returns
with photos
on his phone screen
of the Three Gorges Dam—
the biggest dam in the world,
which chokes the Yangtze River.

He shows them to
all the kids at the table
and the *ayis*,
then moves to the kids
on the floor.

I follow him around
and look at those photos through
three times,
trying to wrap my mind around
all he's seen.

China never does anything by halves,
Toby tells me.

I try to figure out what he means
without asking him,
but then he starts a list:
Great Wall
Forbidden City
Three Gorges Dam
Terracotta Warriors
He counts them off on his fingers.
China is an amazing country.

Is that why you live here?
For the amazingness?
I ask.

Toby smiles slowly.
I'm here for kids like you

and kids who can't help themselves
like Xiao Bo
and Lin Lin,
but I love living in China
just because it's China.
You ought to be proud of your country, Kara.

Opinion

I ask Toby
if we can go in the hall.
That's when I show him
the Gurnseys' letter.

Congratulations!
He side-hugs me.
You've been matched!
His green eyes hold exclamation points
just like his sentences.

Then I show him Mama's letter,
the part about the congressman.

He blows out a big breath.
That's hard, Kara.
I mean, I know they're your family.
He thumps my shoulder too hard.
But people are arguing over you,
that can't be a bad thing, right?

Now I have Toby's opinion,
but it doesn't help.

It should be easy to choose Mama
and the life in Montana, because reaching
her mountains has been my dream
since I was little.

But I worry because
nobody's asked me
what I want,
whether I want a big, matching family
or one familiar mama.

And I'm afraid nobody will.

Portrait

Let me get a shot of you,
Toby says.
Just one
to send home to your American family.

Which family?
I ask.

Toby shrugs.
Maybe both.

I sit on my hands,
look into the camera's
reflective
eye,
force a smile
that's meant
to convince Mama
I'm okay.

I think of Mama
when the light flashes
so bright I blink,
think of Mama
when Toby says,
Great shot,
and leans to show me
myself on the screen:
    a girl
    too skinny
    with long,
    unbrushed
    hair
    and
    no smile
    to be seen.

I thought
I was
smiling.

How Far?

Can I ride my bike
from Tampa
to Bozeman?

Toby laughs.
No idea,
never studied American geography.

We look at the world map
on the wall
in the empty office,
Toby and I
combing the whole USA
with our gaze.

It takes awhile
to find Montana
way up north.

Easier to find Florida
in the south.

So many boxes
in between
with names I can't pronounce, like:
    Alabama
    Mississippi

Oklahoma
Kansas . . .
I imagine mountains
and mountains
and mountains
between them

and my hope
flops.

I thought
I could live in Tampa
and ride my bike to Bozeman
on the weekends.

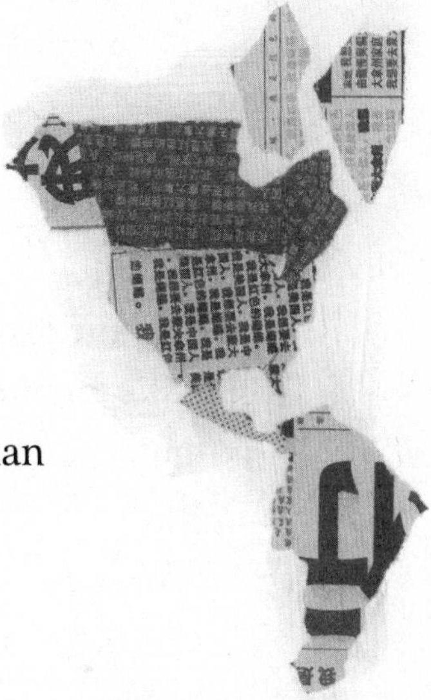

Delay

Toby wants to hear me sing
"Away in a Manger"
just like I'll sing it
in the Christmas show.

After I sing
he says,
Not bad.
You can hold a tune.

But he looks
distracted.

Hey, do you mind
if we walk?
He starts off
fast
before I can answer.

We round the
main building
three times,
    me running,
    Toby's short legs
    going like engine pieces
        right
        left
        right.

Finally he says
quickly,
without looking at me,
I'm afraid your foster parents' actions
have mucked things up a bit.

Chinese officials have to travel to
America to meet with this congressman.

It'll take a while to decide
who you'll go to.

The Gurnseys were ready to come to China
to bring you home
before this happened.

I shove my cold hands
in my pockets,
imagining those big-smile people
crossing the ocean
to take me away.

I say,
But maybe now Mama and Daddy
can take me to Bozeman.

Toby takes a deep breath
and blows it out again.
I don't know if contacting their congressman
will do any good,
to be honest.
All it's managed to do
is slow the whole process,
keep you here longer.

How much longer?
I ask.

Toby shakes his head.
He doesn't know,
nobody does.

I stop at the bathroom,
stand in the farthest stall
from the door,
fumble in my coat pocket
where I stuffed the picture
of the Gurnsey family.

They're still
    smiling
    smiling
    smiling
strangers.

Newspaper Star

Toby rushes into the classroom
where I'm doodling
on lined paper
while the other table kids
    write characters
    row after row
        after row.

Kara, look at this!
He lays a newspaper
covered in English writing
across the table.
The *ayis* lean in to look.

On the front cover
in big black letters it says:

BRING KARA HOME

There I am,
the picture Toby took with his camera.

Where did this come from?
I ask.

It came in the mail for you.
The director's already looked it over.

There I am again,
with Daddy and Jody
in Hangzhou
on a stone bridge.
Daddy holds me,
my thin legs dangling like
puppet legs.

A smaller picture
shows us sitting together
on our living room sofa.
The familiarity of the painting
of limestone peaks in fog
hanging behind our heads,
even the diamond pattern on the old couch,
squeezes my heart with longing.

My hand holding the paper
shakes.

What does it say?
one of the *ayi*s asks.
Even the other kids
look curious enough to speak.

The article says
    how much my parents love me,
    how much they want to bring me
        home to America,
    how difficult it is to adopt
        because of
        all the rules.

It even says Mama's church
where she plays piano
is raising money
for my adoption.

"We're going to make it,"
says a quote from Mama.
"We're going to bring Kara home.
    I can feel it."

Dream

Tonight
I fall asleep
with the newspaper
under my pillow
so no one will take it,
and dream of blue sky
    and a brand-new red bicycle
    that can fly.

If You Were Me

If this were your choice,
who would you live with?
I ask Toby
the next day.

Toby is the safest
person in the world
to ask,
though sometimes he makes jokes.
Like right now:
I've heard the climate in
Florida is fantastic . . .

Toby!
I swat at him,
but he ducks away,
grinning.

All right.
He stops spoon-feeding
Lin Lin
for a moment.

I like it when his eyes
look faraway
because it means
something important
is about to come out of his mouth.

There are good things
about both families.
I know it's hard to imagine,
but I think you'll be happy
in either place
because you're
a happy girl.

I'm feeding
Xiao Bo
porridge
with his favorite
red spoon,
wondering how Toby
can think
I'm a happy girl when
I've been so unhappy.

But I know Mama,
I say,
my throat constricting.
I don't know
those other people.

Toby nods.
Yes, but there are
new beginnings in every life.
As long as you're loved
and safe,
Kara,
you're home.

Hanging On

The Gurnseys send me
another letter.

I sit on the floor
in the hallway
to read it.

This one
does not have
even one single
exclamation point.

Dear Kara,
We wanted you to know why we are hanging on.
We don't want to give up your file
unless we're sure you
can be adopted by your former foster parents.
We want you to be happy,
but we don't want to lose you
to anyone but them.
We'll wait as long as we need to.
Love,
Marilyn & Keith Gurnsey

Truth

After reading the letter,
I sit still,
my back against the hallway wall,

thinking.

Truth
was never something
Mama gave me, but
here these strangers
hand me truth
when they don't even know me,
as if I deserve it.
With Mama
I was always
    too young,
    not ready.
She sheltered me
    until the shelter crashed down
    on both our heads.

I show Toby the letter
and ask,
Is there any chance
for Mama?

Toby eases Lin Lin
into her special seat
and straps her in.

They might have made an exception
to the age rule
if your mum knew the right people.
But since she broke the law
it'll be harder for her to argue her case.

Toby always
gives me truth.

It's like medicine—
hard to swallow,
but good for me.

Holiday

The Christmas program
is scheduled for
December 15
because most of the foreign volunteers
leave on Christmas holiday
  to Phuket,
  Cebu,
  or Panang.

Even Toby is going
to Bali
with his roommate.

You can take care of
Lin Lin and Xiao Bo
while I'm gone,
right?
he asks,
tweaking my nose.
You're becoming an excellent
physical therapist.

His words
warm me
like I'm a radiator
filling with hot water.

I like it,
I say
and I'm not even lying.

The Scarf

The day of the Christmas show,
Toby arrives earlier than usual.

He wears nice clothes,
    a white shirt with thin blue lines
    and a red tie.

He takes me out in the hallway
grinning,

hands me a pink bag
with polka dots,
thin, crumpled paper
poofing from the top.

A present,
he says.
I asked my mum
to make it
specially for you.

I've seen Toby's mum's photo
on his phone:
    her small glasses
    and curly hair
    that sticks up
    in spirals
    all over her head.
His father died when he was small.

I've seen
New Zealand,
where Toby's mum lives,
on the map.
    It's not as big
    as America,
    but Toby says
    it has mountains too.

I carefully remove the
white paper
and pull out
the most beautiful
lavender scarf,
soft
like bird feathers, delicate
like cobwebs.

I cannot
breathe.

Not that I'm a fashion guru,
but I thought it might go well
with the green coat,
Toby says.
You can wear it
when you sing
your song.

I wind the
beautiful
loveliness
around my throat
and say,
I think I'll sing better
with it on.

He has presents
for all the other kids.

Their squeals of delight
echo
into the hallway,
where I remain
to inspect
every detail
of my treasure.

Christmas Show

Miss Li pulls
a small plastic package
from her purse.

Inside is
a butterfly clip
with
red gauze
wings.

For you,
she whispers,
sliding the clip
into my hair.
Thank you for your help
with my English.

I guess I do help
whenever I can,
but not much.

Just pronunciation of words
and the English name I gave her—
Jasmine
because she said she likes flowers
and Jasmine Li
sounded pretty to me.

I am breathless.
Xie xie.

No matter,
she says in English
and clip-clops away
to rub
blush
onto
someone else's
cheeks.

All the kids wear makeup
even if they're only in the choir
or performing little dances
where they dip up and down
or leap in circles.

Even Xiao Bo
wears lipstick
and blush.

He rocks
in a borrowed wheelchair

smiling huge,
head jerking.

The lipstick
I'm wearing
feels sticky,
reminds me
of Mama's
vermilion,
makes me
wonder
about
Zhao Bin,
if he knows what happened to me.

He seems now
part of a whole other life.

My Song

I sing
my song too fast,
because no one
told me
my heart would
leap,
my underarms would
sweat
from all those
staring eyes.

The audience is
mostly ladies
in beige or brown sweaters
with white, smiling faces
and thin, clapping hands.

Toby told me
they're the ones who give money
so that kids can have surgeries
and professionals like Toby
can come
to make the kids' lives
better.

The director beams
from the stage
when the acts are finished.

She declares
it a success:
    all the jumping and leaping
        of the little children,
    all the singing and smiling,
    all the makeup-smeared faces.

We feast on cookies and juice
from a table covered in a
red cloth.
I crumble a cookie
into tiny bits

for Xiao Bo
so he won't choke.

A foreign woman
pats me and says,
Your English is so good!

Her accent is strange.
Toby says it's European.

In Sight

Toby is only here
for two hours today
and then he's going home to pack.

He'll be riding on a big airplane
out of China
to Indonesia.

He showed me
Indonesia
on the map,

a clump of
islands under
the Philippines.

After
only an hour
Miss Li calls him away.

Twenty minutes later
he comes back.

I'm massaging
Lin Lin's cramped feet.
    She smiles
    her tiny-mouthed
    crooked
    smile
    because she likes
    touch.

Kara,
Toby whispers.
The director wants your adoption wrapped up
by Chinese New Year.
You're only one year away from aging out.
She's putting pressure on the authorities
to make a decision about your file.
    The end is in sight.

His words
clang inside me like a cymbal's echo.
    I swing like a pendulum,

one minute
envisioning freedom,
getting out of here
any way I can,
the next remembering
Mama
and realizing
I could wait here
for years
if someone would promise me
her.

Christmas Day

So quiet today.

I'm the only one
at the orphanage
who seems to know
it's special.

I wrap the scarf from Toby's mum
around my neck,
pull on Mama's wool socks,
close my eyes, and
wish for mashed potatoes
and fried chicken
like Mama used to make
on Christmas Day,

then go downstairs
alone
to the cafeteria
to eat cabbage
and boiled peanuts.

Stolen

I've worn
Miss Li's butterfly
every day
since the Christmas show.

It hurt
my head
when I slept,
so I laid it
next to my pillow,
but forgot it
when I got up
to use the bathroom.

I was gone just five minutes, but
when I came back
    it was gone.

Faces

In daylight
I check faces
to find
the mark of a thief:
    averted eyes,
    a haughty toss
    of the head,
    the glimmer of red
    in short black hair.

But every face is
blank,
passive,
    inscrutable.

I play clapping games
with Xiao Bo
extra loud
to cover the throbbing
of my loss.

Breath

I lie awake listening to
    breathing sounds,
        but there's
        one that doesn't fit,

that echoes louder,
every second more intense.

Up on one elbow,
I peer through the dim light
of night in the room.

Labored chokes,
gasp!
huge racking sobs
gasp!

Others are awake,
whites of eyes gleaming in the dark.

Get the ayi*!*
the girl next to me whisper-yells
as if darkness muffles her voice.
It's Xiao Bo.

I pick my way through
the maze of beds.

Xiao Bo
by the window
shudders,
shakes.
He had a cough all day
and wouldn't eat.
Now his skin
burns.

Gone

There is no explanation
when Xiao Bo
doesn't return.
    One day
    two days
    three days
        later.

We ask,
    all of us who can talk,
    ask,
but there's only one answer:
He's at the hospital.

What's wrong with him?

I don't know.

What's he sick with?

We don't know.

Will he ever come back?

. . .

Nothing

I must protect Lin Lin.

Toby depended on me
to watch out
for her
and Xiao Bo.

I failed with Xiao Bo.

I ask the *ayis* if I can
move my bed
next to Lin Lin's,
but they don't let me.

Every day that Xiao Bo is gone
    another stone
    is added
    to my chest.

I only let myself cry
    at night
    when no one else
    can see,
    when the flat pillow
    muffles the sound
    of my fear.

Return

Toby peers
through the doorway
on his first day back
and my heart does three things:
leaps,
shudders, then
plunges.

Kara!
he says.
When I run to him
he tries so hard
to smile.
How are you?

Toby doesn't need to say it.
I see truth written
in the lostness of his eyes,
the way his gaze skitters to the spot
where Xiao Bo used to sit
on the floor,
then skitter back,
attempting to focus on my face,
but failing.

Xiao Bo will never come back.

Small Hope

I cry,
cry,
more than I cried for Mama.
Xiao Bo was my friend, and
in Xiao Bo's smile
hid
a small hope for happy endings.

Now
even that is gone.

Not the First

Sitting at the table,
one of the girls, Yang Zi,
touches my arm,
then withdraws her hand
as if wondering
if touching me
was a mistake.

He's not the first,
she says softly,
continuing to draw
Chinese characters
in boxes
printed on thin paper.
My friend Xing Xing
died last year.

I glance
behind us
at Lin Lin
    rocking
    in her special seat,
smiling
smiling
oblivious.

Dance

Toby stays
until we go to bed.
I think he feels bad
he was gone
when Xiao Bo got sick.

He says good night to me,
then pauses,
second-guessing himself,
before he squats to whisper,
It wasn't anyone's fault,
Kara.
Xiao Bo inhaled a bit of food
that caused pneumonia.

His voice changes, turns
husky.
He's at peace now,
you know.
The place where he is,
he doesn't need to rock
in a wheelchair
when he fancies dancing.
He can stand,
leap,
twirl
all he likes.
Nothing's holding him back.

After Toby leaves,
I close my eyes, only
to spin
all night
hand in hand
with Xiao Bo
in my dreams.

Summons

Mornings,
afternoons pass,
with Xiao Bo's empty space
gaping, but
hours filled
feeding Lin Lin,
drawing pencil marks
on paper, even
daring to trace
the lines
of the Gurnsey family
from the photo,
though they turn out so badly
I throw them away.

It comes suddenly,
the day Toby tells me
with a tremor in his voice,
The director wants to see you.

I am in the middle of feeding
Lin Lin her porridge.

But he makes me hand the bowl to him
and go.

Verdict

The director
sits behind her desk
like a queen,
    elbows propped,
    red lips
    curved
    in a demure
    smile.

Miss Li
stands
to one side
with a notebook,
her pen
tapping.

She's had a haircut.
Her bangs hang in eyes
lined in bright blue
eyeliner.

My stomach
    flips,
    somersaults,
    rolls.
I really have to pee.

Everything has worked out!
the director says
and claps once,
startling me.

I took care of everything,
she continues.
Your new family will be here
for you as soon as possible.

New family?
The words come out in a stammer.
What happened to my—?

No no no,
she says in English,
swishing away my concerns
with a flip of her hand,
her red mouth
still smiling
    smiling.

But why?
The tightness of tears.

The racing
heartbeat
of panic.
Why can't I be with Mama?

The director's smile straightens,
a thin
offended
line.

That situation was impossible,
she snaps.
They are fifteen years older than the age restrictions
and they disobeyed the law.

Impossible,
she repeats.

I stand
on shuddering legs,
reach deep
to find my voice,
    the great,
    booming,
    sure voice,
because if I don't speak
up now
I never will.

WHAT ABOUT ME?

The director nods,
folding one hand
over the other.
What about you, Liu Xiao Ling?
What do you want?

I almost forget
Liu Xiao Ling
is my name,
the official name on paper.
Momentary confusion
makes me blink,
falter.

I try to rally,
gather my courage
because
this is my chance,
to tell her that I want Mama
and mountains
and family
and home
and the familiar

but words don't come
because every hope
has fluttered away
like torn scraps
of translucent paper.

All that's left are disappointments:
Mama forgetting me
when the ambulance door slammed shut;
Daddy standing so still
as they led me away;
the look that passed
between Jody and Willard
when I begged them to keep me.
Inside, I know
nothing will change
if I choose the familiar.
I will always be separate;
someone will always be sorry.

My good hand clutches
the stubby one at my chest.

It's impossible,
I repeat.

The director's smile
returns.
She shuffles papers.
You're a lucky girl.
You'll be happy
in Florida.

Crash

In the hallway,
my heart beats to the tempo
of my regret—
What have I done?
What have I done?
What have I done?

I can never go back,
never go back,
never go
back.

Blindly,
I grab the photo
of the smiling Gurnseys
from my pocket,
rip it
into a thousand pieces.

The bathroom
is an empty,
stinking
place.
The window creaks
when I push it open,
toss out
all those shiny pieces
that glint

in pale sunlight
as they flutter down.

Nothing

There have been packages
from Florida—
    home-baked cookies,
    a purple, sparkly thermos
    that keeps water hot,
    a sweater with a reindeer
    knit onto the front, and,
    the day after I turned twelve,
    a birthday card with glitter and stickers.

But not one letter from Mama.

Tomorrow

I have spent
what feels like years
waiting for spring,
lying in a room
shivering
with other kids
whose coughs
and
wheezes

kept me awake,
    terrified that
    another one of them
    would slip away.

But now
warmth
seeps through
the metal frame
windows.

I begin to think
maybe I won't need
my coat forever.

It happens
the same day
the budding trees
in the orphanage courtyard
fracture
into bloom:

Miss Li
says the dreaded/magic words:
Your new family will be here tomorrow.

Today

A van waits
with Miss Li
and Toby
to take me
to my new family,
who are staying
at the Sheraton Hotel.

There are still days of work ahead—
signing documents,
presentation of papers,
photos,
medical exams.
Then I will get a Chinese passport.

After that we will fly to Guangzhou
to the American Embassy
for a visa.

I will see a different
Chinese city
for the first time
since Hangzhou.

But today,
today I will meet my family.

I should feel excited, but
all I can wish
during my long march
from the front door to the van is that
Mama's face will appear at the gate
so that I can run to her.

The Concept of Good-Bye

The director
stands by the van door,
smiling,
waiting to
pump my hand.

It is a pleasure to meet you,
she says in stilted English.
Then she wishes me
a happy life
in Chinese.

The *ayis*
have brought all the kids
from my room
out,
even though it took
several trips
in the elevator.

I try not to look too deeply
into Yang Zi's
cloudy eyes, fearing
what I'll find there—
hate?
jealousy?
because she told me
she'll never have a family,
that she's almost too old
for adoption.

Watch out for Lin Lin?
I ask,
bending to hug Yang Zi
in her wheelchair.

She nods
into my shoulder,
thin arms
tightening around my neck.

Next, I wrap my arms around
Lin Lin's taught shoulders.
Her mouth hangs open.
She cries in small gasps
and hiccups.

I didn't know
she could understand so much, especially
the concept of good-bye.

Good-Bye, Toby

In the shiny hotel lobby
by the elevator
Toby says,
Maybe it's better if you go on without me.

Here it is:
the end I wouldn't let myself
think about.

I say,
Please come up with me.

But Toby says,
It's time for your new beginning, Kara.
I'll say good-bye here.

I say,
Thank you for everything.
Thank you for . . .
but tears
choke all the words I've been holding.

Toby says,
Shoot me an e-mail when you get settled.
Let me know how you are.
We'll miss you around here.

He holds out his arms for a hug.

He smells different than I expected
close-up,
a smell that reminds me
he's not of the orphanage, but of
far-away mountains,
rivers,
and crisp
blue skies.

Could I visit you and your mum
in New Zealand someday?
I ask.

I'm counting on it.
He ruffles my hair.

He walks away, stooped
as if he carries a mountain
on his shoulders.

At the glass doors,
he turns,
waves a last time.
his mouth moving,
Good-bye.

They All Came

There seem so many of them,
too many
for one small hotel room.

They look like their picture,
but now I hear voices that go
with the smiling faces.

Emily
wears a lavender shirt
with a ballet slipper on it.

Rosalie
has a red flower in her hair
with a sparkly center.

The red of it matches
my butterfly clip
that is gone.

And the boys—
David and Ethan
are so tall,
taller than their
mother and father,

who are now my mother and father.

But I can't think of that now, because
the idea might
crumble
me.

I shake hands
with each of them
and they say,
Hey
or
Hi
or
Nice to meet you.
My left hand shakes their right hands,
my other hand
carefully
hidden
inside my sleeve.

Their mother pulls me into a hug,
crying wet tears
that smear my cheek,
her thick sweater
soft against my face,
her smell like a flower market
in summer,
not a motherly smell
at all.

Please, she says,
let me take your bag.
Do you want to rest?
Do you want anything to eat?
To drink?

They all
look so beautiful,
like movie stars,
especially Emily,
with her
pink shimmery lips
that are better than vermilion red.

Will I ever fit with this
glamorous family of
Gurnseys?

With a pang
I miss
Mama's
quiet ways,
her measured
gait,
her soft
voice,
familiar
supple
clothes
worn
thin.

Rescue

Maybe my eyes look
startled
or sad
from all the commotion,
because Mr. Gurnsey says,
Let's not
overwhelm her, kids.
Go back to your own
rooms
and give Kara
a minute.

But you told us we had to be in here
to say hello.
Emily has a whiny
voice that sounds like
it belongs to one
of the little kids
from the orphanage's
lower floors.

There'll be plenty of time
for getting to know each other,
he answers,
no-nonsense firm.

The kids,
my new sisters and brothers,
file out.

Miss Li
smiles
when the room is quiet
and gives directions
for the next few days.

While the translator translates
I sit straight on the edge of the bed,
letting my backpack
slide from my shoulders, but
still holding
tight to the handle

because it feels
as if my old life
is fluttering
away,
every shred of it.

Mrs. Gurnsey

She
tucks me
under hotel sheets,
my backpack cuddled
next to me.

What's in there?
she asks.

Books,
I whisper.

Oh?
Which ones?

Pride and Prejudice
is the only title I can remember
right now,
my brain
a whirling
fog.

I've been meaning to read that
for years,
she says.

Me too,
I say.

I've seen the movie
several times,
she says.

There's a movie?

She nods.

A movie in English?

She laughs.
Quite a few movies, actually.
And yes, they're in English.
What if we read your book together?

I nod,
a slow
warm trickle
of hope
filling my chest.

That would be fine.

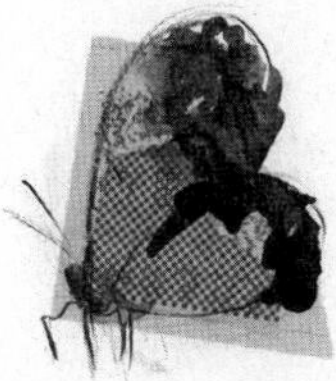

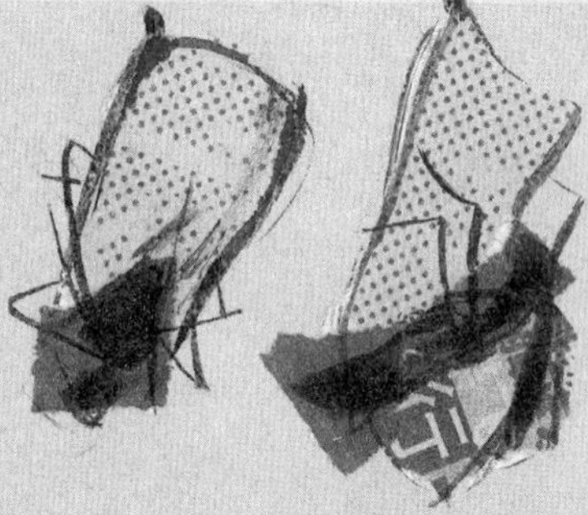

Part Three

Fly

A Window to the World

I watch the earth fall away,
watch everything big turn
tiny.

A race of small vehicles,
weave of roads,
curve of rivers,
wedge of
shimmering canals.

I press my nose to the cold glass,
straining to make out—
    that is where I walked,
    that is where I rode my bike,
    there is our apartment,
or is it a neighborhood that looks
just like ours?
I can't be sure.

All I know is
    I'm flying.

Now the city fades
behind a haze of clouds
that from below looked cottony,
but are actually thick air.

Tianjin,
my city, vanishes
beneath us
and there is nothing yet
to replace it.

Torn Paper

Their kids are in other rows,
    two here,
    two there.
Mr. and Mrs. Gurnsey sit with me.

The boys play games
on their phones.

The girls pore
over books filled with pictures
of beautiful girls' faces
    with stickers of earrings
    bracelets
    hair bows
and argue over the prettiest jewelry.

Mrs. Gurnsey gave me a book too,
but I'm saving mine, wondering
if she'll let me
mail it to Yang Zi

so she can decorate
the girls herself
and show the pictures
to Lin Lin.

Mrs. Gurnsey rests her warm hand on my back
as she leans to look out the window.
There goes Tianjin.
Will you miss it?

I nod once,
wishing I could shrug away her hand
without being rude.
I cannot explain how my emotions
are split down the middle, like
a piece of paper torn
in two:
missing Tianjin,
hating Tianjin,
the home of my happiness and
of my loss.

Fast

In the Guangzhou hotel room,
I sit on the windowsill
and run my fingernail over the
air-conditioning grate.

It makes a sound like an instrument,
this way going higher,
this way going lower.

Cool air poufs out my hair,
blows under the sleeve of my shirt.

I sit still.

Everyone else moves
so fast,
clattering,
talking.
The girls argue
because they want to go shopping
now!

More noise
than the fifteen children
crammed in the large room
I left behind.

Made in China

When the girls come back
from shopping
they're giggling, heads
tucked together like
nesting pigeons.

You show her.

No, you show her.

No, you.

Rosalie trips forward,
pushed by Emily.

We got one for all three of us,
she says.
Look!

She unfurls
a T-shirt
rolled into a
white ball.

MADE IN CHINA
say red words across the chest.

She laughs.
We're all three made in China,
get it?

Mrs. Gurnsey on the bed
props herself on one elbow.
She looks tired when she says,
Maybe Kara doesn't understand.

In America it's a joke,
Mr. Gurnsey says,
that everything people buy at the store
is made in China.

I feel like he's saying
I'm a joke.
I want to pull
the curtains over myself
and hide against the windowsill.

Emily sulks at my silence,
tosses the T-shirt
on the bed,
and says,
We were just joking around.
It's not like we have to wear them.

I turn my eyes
out the window
to stare at this China that
looks nothing like
my China,
to the wide, blue river

that is nothing like
the straight canals
I've always known.

I don't fit with these Americans.

I don't want to go
to America
to become a joke.

Mismatch

Mrs. Gurnsey wants me to wear new clothes
to the embassy,
clothes she brought from America.

    Emily, Rosalie and I
    all have the same shirt,
    but in three different colors:
        red
        blue
        green.

I get green.

After we're dressed
Mrs. Gurnsey lines us up
in front of the mirror.

My gorgeous girls,
she says, smiling.

Emily with her shiny hair and sparkling eyes,
Rosalie with her lip gloss,
and me
    raggedy hair hanging long down my back,
    face puffy,
    arm sticking out
    without a full hand on the end.

In the orphanage
    at least I looked
    like I fit.

Shame

I don't want to match,
I say,
snatching the long-sleeved shirt
I wore on the day I left the orphanage
from the top of the suitcase.

I rush to the bathroom
and shut the door.

With a long sleeve I can cover my hand
so people at the embassy won't stare,
won't take one look at me and know
that's why I'm here.

Maybe Mrs. Gurnsey wanted Chinese triplets,
but I will never be like them,
    my smile as big,
    my hair as beautiful,
and I'll never have two hands.

Mrs. Gurnsey knocks.
    I know it's her
    because Mr. Gurnsey would
    knock louder and say,
    Open up.

I don't want her to
come in
because I don't want to explain
why
the shirt she picked out
sits in a heap on the
tiled floor.
But she comes in anyway.
Don't you like the color, Kara?
It looks great with your skin tone.

I shake my head.

What's your favorite color, honey?

It's not the color.

Then what's the problem?

She should know
like Mama always knew.
I never had to explain
anything
to Mama.

My hand,
I say.

Mrs. Gurnsey shuts the door.
You're embarrassed of your hand?

I need long sleeves.

Mrs. Gurnsey reaches out,
but I back up,
shoulder to the wall.

I'll remember that,
she says softly.

Embassy

I'm the oldest one
getting an American visa today.

All the other parents
have black-haired baby girls
with pigtails

or little kids
in squeaky sneakers
who run in circles
watching their reflections
in the shiny
marble floor.

But one little boy
has a body bent
in a C shape.

He reminds me of a younger Xiao Bo,
the way he holds his hand
like a claw.

His father
cradles him and
I think how Xiao Bo
would have liked
to be held like that, a treasure
someone longed for.

Official

I wish Mama were here.
I'd like to tell her,
Look,
I'm finally becoming
what you always told me
I was.

Look,
I have a name
written in an official book
and official parents
and an identity to prove it.

Look,
I'm somebody's child
on my way to America.

Now
if only I could feel it.

Family Picture

Outside the embassy
we stand
clustered on the road
while
Mrs. Gurnsey argues
with Mr. Gurnsey about
where to take the
family picture.

Finally
we crowd together
in front of a bank of dusty shrubs,
Mr. Gurnsey's choice,

Ethan and David flanking their parents
because they're so tall,
the three of us girls in front.

I hide
my arm
behind
Emily's back
without touching her.

Mrs. Gurnsey asks
another
adopting family
to take our picture.

A man
with hardly any hair
takes the camera,
his wife holding
a baby girl with one eye
bigger than the other,
wearing a yellow bow
as large as her head.

The baby is not
happy
or sad.
She only observes us
as if we're a television show.

I wish I were
like her,
too young to know
what's happening.

That's how I was
with Mama and Daddy.
All I knew was them.

My stomach aches,
because of the strangers
lined up behind me,
next to me,
pretending to be my family.
It should be Mama and Daddy
standing on either side,
arms threaded through mine.
I can't let Mrs. Gurnsey's burning hands
touch me, as if
I belong to her, as if
    Mama never was.

Deep Purple

Rosalie
shakes a bottle of purple
nail color
so it goes

click
click
click.

In the hotel bathroom I sit
on the white tub rim,
Rosalie on the
closed toilet.

Give me your hand,
she says,
so I hold out my good hand.

I've never
ever
had my nails painted,
but I remember
all the beautiful women
in *People* magazine
with long, elegant fingers
and nails like rainbows.

When she looks at my hand
she makes a face
and says,
Kind of ragged,
then shrugs.
Oh well.

Emily perches on the counter
beside the sink,
legs folded beneath her.
For a moment,
I can almost touch
the idea
that we are sisters,
but then it slips away.

Wait till you see our house,
Emily says.
Wait till you see your room.
We've been decorating
for months.
Literally.

When are you going to start school?
Rosalie asks.
Have you ever gone to school before?

I shake my head.

Never?
Emily says.
Lucky.

It's okay,
Rosalie says.
You're twelve, right?
Em and I are too. For now.

I'm almost thirteen.
You can meet all our friends,
but I'll be a grade ahead of you,
probably.

You're older than me.
Emily sticks out her lower lip.
It's not fair.
I always have to be the youngest.
But I get the impression
she doesn't actually mind.

Rosalie is good with the nail polish brush,
stroking smooth
    thick
    lines.
My whole nail looks black
at first,
drying slowly to purple.
I think
it looks pretty
against my pale skin.

Do you play basketball?
Emily asks.

No.

Do you do anything?

Ride my bike.

But what about sports?

I shake my head.

You don't do anything?

I do physical therapy.

Emily screws up her face.
What does that even mean?

History

Later, Rosalie lies
next to me
on her stomach,
just the two of us,
shoulders brushing,
her legs striking the mattress
as she kicks
flop
plop
flop.

I was five when Mom and Dad got me,
she says.
Emily was a baby.
Well, she was nearly two.

You were five?
I imagined them as twins,
but not twins,
carried out of the orphanage together.

Yes. I have spina bifida,
an opening in my spinal cord,
but when I was little
I had a surgery
to fix it.

I catch my breath,
remembering something
Toby told me.
My friend Yang Zi
had that too—
an opening in her spine!

The excited words pour out
before I remember
that Yang Zi also had surgery.
But . . .
she can't walk.

Rosalie twists her hair
into a ball
fluidly
and slides in a clip to hold it.
Yep, I was lucky.

Rosalie's feet *thump-thump,*
her fingers interweave,
until she says,
I remember a little when Mom and Dad
came to get me,
but Em doesn't.
She knows them
like she's always been with them.

I try to tell if Rosalie's saying
more than she's saying.
I wonder if she's saying
    she understands
    better than Em
    what it's like
    to be me.

Arrival

We're here.

It's hard to
figure out
what Florida
is like
from the air:
buildings
set in rows
and roads

crisscrossing,
crawling with
so many tiny cars.

On the ground,
we load up in
the Gurnseys' big van
and everyone
gushes,
It's good to be home!
But Em says,
Our van is dusty,
and makes a disgusted face.

Outside the window flashes
blue water,
so much blue water
I think we must
be crossing another ocean
on a bridge that never ends.

But then the bridge does end,
and the van sails along
wide, smooth roads
rimmed in
brilliant green trees,
narrow white paths
that are sidewalks
as clean as if
nobody ever walked on them,
blue sky
as if nobody ever
breathed on it.

Mrs. Gurnsey glances back at me
and says,
We'll go to the beach
as much as we like!
Especially when Grandma
comes to visit this summer!
And Rosalie says,
And we'll take Kara to Busch Gardens
and Disney World!

But I close my eyes, wondering
if Montana is the same
as this,
if it can possibly be
as clean,
as beautiful, and
how long do I have to wait
until I can go there?

Drive Through

You've eaten here before, right, Kara?
Mr. Gurnsey says,
pulling into a parking lot,
then a narrow road
with other cars lined up.

The kids are all starving.
At least,
that's what they say:
I'm starving!
I'm starving!

He rolls down his window
in front of a lighted board
covered in pictures
of food.

What do you all want?
he calls over his shoulder.

The rest of them know:
burgers
fries
Em wants ice cream

How about you, Kara?
he asks.

I know this place
with its big yellow *M*,
but I'm too embarrassed to say
I only ate here once
and didn't like it,
that if I eat one of those
piled-up white ice cream cones
I might throw up
all over their beautiful
(dusty)
van.

House

The Gurnseys' house
is down a white, winding drive
rimmed in funny trees
with long, smooth trunks,
prickly leaves
sprouting from their tops.

I think the house is a hotel
until Mr. Gurnsey stops the van
close to it
and says,
Home sweet home.

The front door makes a
bleeping noise when you open it,

and the ceiling soars
up
up
up
to a high, round place
where a hanging light
shimmers with shards of colored glass.

Downstairs there's
a room with a big table,
colored balls scattered
that you can roll with your hand
or plunk with a stick.
    (If you use the stick
    be careful not to scrape
    the green fabric.)

There is a swimming pool
through a door in the back
surrounded
by windows

so sunshine
pours in.

Mr. Gurnsey asks
if I know how to swim.

I shake my head,
unwilling to tell him
that even the bathtub
at the hotel
scared me.

My room is
down a hallway
with carpet soft as cloud.
Em is on one side,
Rosalie on the other,
Mr. and Mrs. Gurnsey
at the end.
The boys are in
the other wing,
Mrs. Gurnsey says.

My wall
has purple birds flying
    that make me think
    of Jim the bird,
    which makes me think
    of Daddy.

There are statues of birds
nestled on the shelves too.
They look so real,
if I reach out to them,
I'm sure they'll duck away
and dive for the sparkling window.

It's beautiful here.
My heart shudders with excitement,
but I tell it not
to make a racket
about pretty things.
    This isn't home.
    It can't be.

I won't trade Mama for a palace,
no matter how much
Mrs. Gurnsey smiles and
squeezes my shoulder and
gazes at me with hopeful eyes.

I don't want to hurt her, but
how can I live
in the same country as Mama
without being close to her?

Quiet

After the room of kids
at the orphanage
and the small rooms
in the hotel,
the Gurnsey's giant house
has so much quiet.

I can't even hear Mr. Gurnsey snore
like I could
through the thin hotel walls.
I can't hear
anyone.

When I close my eyes,
listening to silence,
I can believe
I'm the only one left
in the entire world.

Jet Lag

I wake up
expecting early morning,
but find brilliant day
and the clock saying
noon.

I roll over,
eyes muddy,
brain wanting to sleep
a hundred more years.

The bed is a cloud
to sink into.
It pulls you in, fades
you away
before you realize
you're sleeping.

It makes you dream
before you realize
you're dreaming.

I wonder if Mama's bed in Montana
could be as comfortable as this.
Is it disloyal
that I forgot about Mama
while I slept?

Dinner

Mrs. Gurnsey taps on my door
that evening.
Come to dinner?
A hopeful question,
not a command.

Dinner is louder
because we're all together
in a special room
just for eating.

Ethan and David went
back to school
today.

David is tired,
taps his forehead on the table
and says,
Jet lag stinks.

Mrs. Gurnsey
reminds the girls
they'll go back tomorrow.

What about Kara?
Emily asks.

I pay attention to the answer
because it's
something I want to know too.
Even though we're all twelve,
I feel smaller than Rosalie and Em, somehow.
Stupider, for sure.

Mrs. Gurnsey hums like she's thinking,
but then the answer comes out decided:

We'll keep you out
till next school year,
just so you have longer to settle.
Is that okay with you?

I nod,
because it is okay.
    I'm desperately curious,
    but everything I know of school
    is the outside of gray buildings
    labeled with long strings of
    Chinese words,
    and students filing in
    with red scarves tied at their collars.
I cannot imagine
Florida school,
all these glamorous
American kids in bright clothes
congregating in one place.
Even imagining
is terrifying.

No fair,
Emily mutters.
She seems so determined
to compare our two worlds,
to make everything so even
between us,
so silvery smooth.

I think she'd like to see
her own reflection
when she looks at the Gurnsey family:
everything,
everyone
focused only
on
her.

Lasagna

We're eating something called
lasagna:
    fat noodles
    too much cheese
    tomato sauce

Do you like the food?
Mrs. Gurnsey asks,
hopeful,
hovering.

It's great.

I cannot hurt
Mrs. Gurnsey.
She cares so much, wearing
all her caring
on her face
all the time.

I cannot tell her
how the heavy smells,
the thickness of American food
make my stomach churn
and puff out
like a balloon.

School

After breakfast
the next morning
Mrs. Gurnsey takes everyone
to school.

I ride
in the very back
since
I don't need to climb out.
I like it back here,
curled up in my quiet corner.

When Mrs. Gurnsey stops at the curb,
Em and Rosalie
bound out
of the van
and instantly
meet
a friend
with straw-colored hair
and sparkly eyes.

They link arms,
cross the street
to the school building—
a place with arched doorways
and an American flag
hanging limp from a pole.

I try to imagine myself
here
someday,
walking into that
big
building,
my head tipped back,
so sure of myself.

But that kind of imagining
still gives me a headache.

Mrs. Gurnsey glances back.
We have the whole day
to ourselves.
Want to do something special?

I already know what to say,
as if I've been waiting for the question
since I arrived in Florida.

The beach,
I say.
I've never been to one.

Mrs. Gurnsey's face brightens
like I've handed her a present.

The Beach

With every step, I
sink
into the sand a little.

There's dry, sliding sand
away from the water
and sticky, wet sand
where the waves rush in.

Those waves have foamy teeth
that nibble my toes.
I laugh,
spring away,
because it tickles.

Slap
slap
slap
go my bare feet
when I run.
Shrieking birds
circle overhead.

Behind me shine
sloppy footprints.

Mrs. Gurnsey
takes my left hand,
her laugh rippling
over the
bright waves,
the silky wind,
as if she's
never felt
the scrub of sand
between her toes
before.

Want ice cream?
she asks.

Ice cream.
Jody.
Mama.

A cloud
wanders
in front of the sun.

My stomach starts to hurt, because
I don't know if Mama
has ever seen the ocean like this.
And I don't know
if we'll ever see it together.

I want to go back to your house,
I say,
watch the light
go out of Mrs. Gurnsey's eyes.

I want to explain, but
I can't make my mouth form words.
    How a place so beautiful
    can make me feel so sad.

Nothing

Mrs. Gurnsey *tap tap taps*
on the door of my silent
alone
room.

I'm so tired
after the beach,
so tired of trying
so hard
not to hurt her,
I don't care
anymore.

Kara,
she whispers.
What are you doing in here?
It's so dark.

Nothing.

Do you want to read
Pride and Prejudice *together?*
I'm not doing anything . . .

No.

Do you need more books to read?
We could go to the library?

No.
Thank you.

Her breath comes sharp.
Maybe . . .
Would it help . . . ?
I was wondering . . .

I trace an endless line
on my bedsheets
with my fingertip,
    a line with dips,
    jags,
    and angles.

There's still some purple
left on the nail of my index finger,
    just a tiny bit,
    so dark
    it looks black.

Would you like to call your foster parents?
She says it quickly
as if afraid
slow words won't make it out of her mouth.

Eager

Every day
I ask,
Today?

There's always an answer
that means
"not quite yet."

Either
I'm waiting to hear back from . . .
or
I haven't gotten a hold of . . .

Until the day comes
when Mrs. Gurnsey says,
We'll call them after lunch today.

She shows me the laptop,
how it will work,
how we'll call Montana.
I sit in front of the screen
waiting,

barely touching the sandwich
she puts in front of me
with folded meat and lettuce inside.
My stomach
distracts me with its fluttering.

I'll really be able to see Mama?
I ask.

Right on that screen,
Mrs. Gurnsey says, pointing.
I wish I didn't notice
how anxious she is.

And she wants to talk to me?
I ask.

Well, of course she does.
Mrs. Gurnsey says,
her brow contracting in confusion.
Why wouldn't she?

I shrug.
But inside, I worry
Mama hasn't written
or called until now
because she's disappointed
in me.

Through the Screen

They are on the screen,
    their faces,
    their voices,
Mama and Daddy
with Jody squeezed in
just like Mrs. Gurnsey said
they'd be.

And there I am,
    a little face
    looking back
    from the screen corner.

You've grown a bunch,
Mama says.
Your face has changed.

I don't know if she means
    worse
    or
    better.
It's hard to tell
through a screen.

The old disappointment
creeps up on me—
that this is not,

cannot be
the same.

Mama's voice sounds different,
brittle, like
a broken peppermint
crunched in the wrapper.

Tampa's being good to you?
Daddy asks.
The weather's nice down there, I hear.

Jody's face
fills the screen when she leans forward.
Are they being good to you?
Treating you well?

Daddy and I moved to Missoula
to be close to Jody,
Mama says.
We're managing an apartment complex.
We live on the bottom floor.

It's pretty nice.
There's a washer and a dryer
and Daddy fixes things when they're broke.
Only thing is,
we have to be ready any time of night
if anyone calls.

Not easy on this old man,
let me tell you,
Daddy says,
grinning.
But it sure beats the security guard
hours I used to work.

The place smells like mildew,
Jody says,
but it's bigger than what you had in China.

Noisier neighbors,
Daddy says.

It feels like they're
filling up the empty space
between us
with lots of words,
the same kind of noise
Jody always brought
when she visited,
all the noise I wanted her
to take away
when she left.

Through the screen
there's no such thing
as companionship.

Mama won't remind me to do chores
or fold my clothes
or ask me to bring her a cup of water.
Through the screen
I can't even bring myself to ask
why she stopped writing.

We miss you, sugar,
Mama says
in that crumbly peppermint voice.

I miss you too.
But not just talking,
I want to say how
I miss being.
How I miss knowing
exactly
what Mama's feeling.

But saying that
wouldn't make any sense
through the screen.

Lies

Okay?
Mrs. Gurnsey asks
after I shut the laptop.

She's been standing there, listening
and chopping onions,
    endless onions,
while I talked to Mama and Daddy.

That one word
    okay?
(or maybe it's the way she says it,
like everything should be okay now
that I've gotten my way)
weaves a sharp strand of anger
through all the sadness that
has bound itself
like a nest of protection
around my heart.

It was fine,
I say, because
    if I tell her
    how disappointed I am
    she might never
    let me talk to them
    again.

There's a brochure here,
she says,
for summer rec.
She scoots a yellow booklet
across the counter.
The girls will be doing activities.
I wondered if you'd be interested.

I can't do sports.
I hold up my hand
as a reminder,
because sometimes Mrs. Gurnsey
seems to think
she can fix every single
thing that's wrong.
And she can't.

Sure you can,
she says.
You can do anything you put your mind to.

Not catch a ball.

Sure you could catch a ball.

Not play piano.

Yes, even play piano.

I turn away,
    feel the weight of her
    determination
    boring into my back.
There's nothing I want more
than to get away
from her and
the truth
that she's lying to me.

Mystery

While the girls are at school the next day,
I sneak into the front room,
which smells of peonies,
the fancy room with high windows,
a pale blue couch,
and a palm tree in a glazed pot.

A ceiling fan rotates overhead
with blades shaped like big leaves.
Palm fronds stir,
miniature versions of the tall palms outside.

This place feels almost too beautiful to stand in and
I doubt I'm allowed to be in here
at all

because everything
looks as if it could break.

The huge piano
stretches sleek black,
the lid tipped up so I can peek inside
at taught strings shining gold.

I touch the keys
white white
black white black,
but don't dare press them down,
not yet,
because the sound
may not be soft as flower petals on silk,
    it might be loud,
    obnoxious,
    dream-shattering.

Someone's music
propped up
looks like the beautiful script
of a different language:
black lines, circles, curlicues.

I know it all means
something, a code
waiting to be figured out.

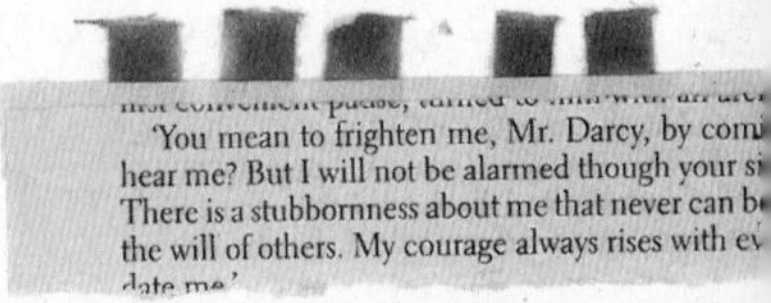

'You mean to frighten me, Mr. Darcy, by com
hear me? But I will not be alarmed though your s
There is a stubbornness about me that never can b
the will of others. My courage always rises with e

Question

Who plays your piano?
I ask Mrs. Gurnsey.

She looks up
from a plugged-in mop
that lets out steam
in a whoosh.

Emily takes lessons,
she says.
I tried to convince Rosalie,
but she's too preoccupied
with sports.

I can't imagine
someone with two hands
not wanting to play
a luxurious
piano
that sits in a front room
all day and night waiting
to be played.

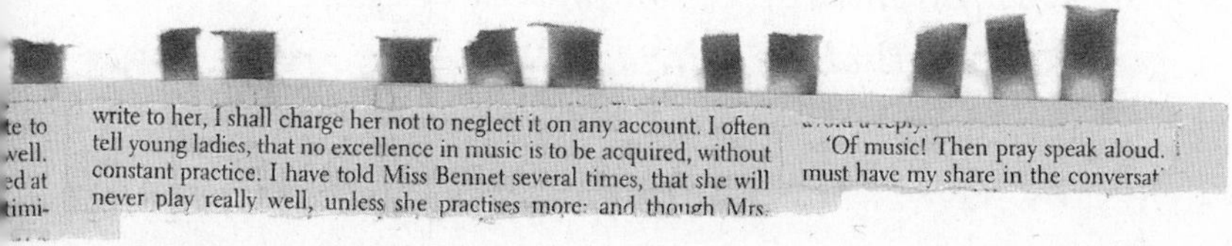

write to her, I shall charge her not to neglect it on any account. I often
tell young ladies, that no excellence in music is to be acquired, without
constant practice. I have told Miss Bennet several times, that she will
never play really well, unless she practises more: and though Mrs.
'Of music! Then pray speak aloud.
must have my share in the conversat

Visiting Hour

I visit Mama and Daddy almost
every day,
hunched close to the screen
trying to catch every glimpse of their life
to see if anything familiar remains.

It's never enough,
but it's better than nothing.

My biggest fear is
we'll run out of things to say.

Instead of talking,
I want to see Daddy
kiss Mama's cheek,
hear the door slam
when he goes to fix someone's apartment,
smell the mildew,
hear the tumble of the washing machine
and know our clothes are in there,
hear Mama singing
in the shower
through the thin walls,
my feet propped up on an old coffee table,
    reading *Pride and Prejudice*
        page
    by page
by page.

I'll never fit here
in this house with too many doors,
long hallways,
and steps on carpet so thick
my foot makes no sound,
where everything seems
perfect,
from the
neat green grass expanses
to the front room
with its slow-moving, dustless fan.

Mama and me,
we were so connected,
every breath
taken together.
    Here, everyone moves
    to a separate rhythm,
    confined to a large
    personal space.
    I've never been so
    alone.

Afraid

Mrs. Gurnsey asks
if I've picked a summer activity
from the book yet.

No, I say.
There's nothing I want to do.

What about puppeteering
or drama
or a poetry workshop?
You don't have to do sports.

No.

She tells me I've got to try.

No.

Then what's the point?
she asks.
You're going to sit in your room
all day alone,
reading?
That will be your life?

I can tell she's angry though
trying to be gentle,
pushing her feelings down
so her words are soft,
though they cut like jagged glass, because
    I still haven't read
    a single page
    even though I pretend to
    every day.

Are you afraid to settle here?
she asks.
Are you afraid of liking it?

No,
I say,
my teeth gritted as if I'm lying,
though I'm not sure I'm lying.
I'm not sure of anything,
just that being here makes
    my insides squirm,
    my shoulders tighten up to my ears,
    my lips smash together.

Maybe for a while,
she says,
we should leave off calling Montana.

My head snaps around.
No.

We're your forever family,
she says,
crouching close to me.
I know it's hard to let go of what you had,
but we want you here.
We—

No,
don't make me . . .

But I can't finish.
I race for the stairs,
slam my door
so hard
the whole
    quiet
    house
    shudders.

Library

The next morning
after everyone has been dropped off
    and all the work
    Mrs. Gurnsey
    does to fill her time
    has been done,
she takes me to the library
    to rooms of books,
    millions of pages of stories,
and says,
Pick whatever you want.

But I don't know what I want.
It's like standing in an
American supermarket
staring at rows of cereal
    knowing milk gives me a stomachache.

Pick anything,
Mrs. Gurnsey says.

But I stand still so long,
uncertain,
that she finally snatches books about
polar bears
pianos
piranhas
from the juvenile nonfiction shelves
and says,
Let's go,
really short.

I climb back in
the big, gold van
with seats for us all
that squeak when I slide
across them.
I catch her eyes in the mirror
watching me,
calculating her
disappointment.

Less Than Empty

Every morning
I wake
with a single thought:
This will be the day
Mrs. Gurnsey will crack,
    let me open the computer again,
    let me see Mama's face,
    let me hear her voice.

But she never cracks.

Every visit left me wanting,
but every day without visits
    is a desert without light,
    less than empty.

Ungrateful

Emily comes home
from an end-of-year party
at a friend's house
and all she can talk about is
everything
Jolie
has.

Jolie has
    a basset hound puppy,
    prettier bedroom furniture,
    a Wii in her room,
    all the dolls from American Girl,
    an entire wall of
    beauty contest crowns.

Emily stomps at dinner,
says she hates ravioli
more than anything in the world—
    the grossest food
    ever made
    for human consumption.

Rosalie groans,
but that only makes
Em madder.

Mrs. Gurnsey says,
There are so many people
in the world
with hardly anything, Em.
Try to be grateful.
Her compassionate eyes
rest on me.

I wasn't talking about the whole world,
Em yells,

stomping from the table
and up the stairs.
I was talking about myself!

Mrs. Gurnsey trails,
standing at the bottom step
calling,
Come on, Em.
Please,
don't overreact.

But Em
doesn't come back.

The house
falls
to silence
    of boys sending texts
    and listening to music
    through earbuds,
    of Rosalie staring at her plate,
    slapping tomato sauce
    with her fork.
I cower, knowing
Em's anger has something to do with me.

It was the way she glared
before she launched herself up the stairs.
She wasn't thinking about Jolie anymore.
All her eye-fire
flew at me.

Tidal Wave

After dinner
Rosalie
    hurries upstairs.
I creep back to my room, but
in the hallway I
pause outside the cracked-open door
of Em's room,
stopped
by the sound
of their voices.

Em lies
facedown
on her purple bedspread.

She turns her face,
a red splotch on each cheek.
    Everything's about Kara!

I shrink against the shadowy wall,
ready to slink away.
But then Rosalie says,
Not everything.

Yes, everything!
Em insists.
She's the only one
Mom cares about!

She's not even careful
to be quiet,
as if she wants
the whole house to know
how much she hates me.
Mom walks around
crying all day,
worrying about Kara!

Well, Kara's new
and she's had a hard life,
Rosalie says.

A streak of resentment
cuts through me,
even though I like Rosalie, because
how does she know
anything about my life?
Most of it was good,
for her information.

Em grunts into the pillow.

Mom loves you
and you know it,
Rosalie says.

But I want our family
to be the same as before,
Em wails.
Before SHE came.

Something breaks
in me, a
tidal wave of anger.

I sweep past the door,
not bothering to hush.
I don't mind the whole house knowing
that I heard proof of
    Emily's resentment.

Aftermath

Rosalie knocks on my door.
I know it's her
because she taps
with her fingernails.

I don't ask her to come in,
    which may be mean,
    but I can't stand
    being with anyone
    right now.
    Even her.

Em acts spoiled sometimes,
but she's not really,
she says through the door.
    She just . . .
    She just . . .
    feels insecure.

I don't know what
Em could be insecure about.
Rosalie is making
excuses
so I'll feel better.

Either way,
I don't answer.
    Sometimes silence
    is better at speaking anger
    than a thousand words.

Pack

Pack a bag,
leave everything
the Gurnseys ever gave me
behind.

What I pack
is almost the same
as what I took
to the hospital that day
a different lifetime ago,
    except now there's the scarf from Toby.

In Montana,
it'll be cool enough
to wear it.

The Plan

There's a way of finding out
what you want to know,
but don't want to ask.

This way is called
Google.

I watched Rosalie
use it one time,
typing on the screen of her iPad
to find directions to the water park
where her friend
was having a party.

> (She said I could come,
> said it would be fun.
> But I didn't want to;
> I've seen the things people
> wear when they swim.)

I pull my iPad
from its cover,
press the button,
watch the screen blink awake.

All I have to do is type at the top
H-O-W
D-O

I
G-E-T
T-O
M-O-N-T-A-N-A,
letters one by one,
then wait for the ticking screen
to spit out
the answer.

Cheap flights!
Cheap flights!
Cheap flights!
    that aren't so cheap.

Greyhound bus:
Two days
Twelve hours
Twenty minutes
Two hundred and fifty dollars

Mr. and Mrs. Gurnsey
give me money
they call "allowance"
every Sunday.

I empty it
on the bedspread
and count
to ninety.

They said I should
    save some,
    spend some,
    give some away.

But there's only
one thing
I want.
It will take
six more weeks
to save up
the one hundred and sixty
extra dollars
to get to Missoula
by bus,
with twenty more
for food and emergencies.

I shove my filled-up
backpack
under the bed,
shift the bed skirt
to scrape the floor
so no one can see it,
stuff the money
back in the purse
Mrs. Gurnsey gave me,
take out the calendar
with kittens
Mrs. Gurnsey gave me,

and count
six more weeks,
two days.

Granola

Every other day
I sneak
a granola bar
from the cupboard
and slide it into
my backpack
under the bed.

Granola bars
are wonderful choices:
instant food
in a tiny,
concealable
package.

Summer

When the school year ends,
the house has noise
all day
    with Emily's piano playing
    and Rosalie and the boys splashing in the pool
    in the slanting rays of light,
    their cell phones perched on deck chairs.

The boys have loud voices.
Rosalie shrieks when they toss her.
    The water sploshes,
    waves crashing
    over the concrete edge.

I stand beside the glass door
watching them
and although Rosalie motions for me to come
I shake my head,
ducking sideways so she can no longer
see me lingering in the shadows.

Besides,
    I like to hear the sound
    of the piano's soft flutter
    from the other room.

Even if it is Em playing.

Luck

She's so lucky.
Em's voice
makes me jump.

We watch Rosalie
swim like a koi fish,
slip away from the boys
like she's slick with scales.

I'm not sure
why Em
would think
Rosalie is luckier
than she is.

I'm not even sure
why Em
is talking
to me.

Even though it was a week ago,
the memory of what
she said
forces my body
stiff.

She's nice,
I say
stubbornly,

remembering that
Rosalie
stood up for me.

Em shrugs.
And lucky.

A flare of anger
makes me brave.
You're lucky too.

Em screws up her face.
You'd never catch me
wearing that suit.

Why not?

Because people would see my scar,
she says.
Unless I wear an old-lady suit,
which I'm not willing to do.
Rosalie's scar is on her back,
and nobody looks at your back.

I didn't know Em had a scar,
but I say,
It shouldn't matter
about your scar
if you're with your family.

It's ugly,
she says.
I'd rather play the piano
. . . fully clothed.

Where is your scar?
I ask.

You mean you don't know?
Rosalie didn't tell you?

I shake my head.

Well, if you have to know.
She rolls her eyes
    in a way that makes me think
    she was waiting for me to ask
and yanks down her shirt collar.

A fat pink line
descends down the center
of her chest.

There.
Happy?

What happened?
I ask.

Open-heart surgery
when I was two,
she says.
I was a blue baby.

Brave

I'm still mad at Em.
But something else
slowly
bites away my anger.

She has fears too.
   It's hard to hate her
   when we're so much alike.

Reading

I stare at Mama's curling, happy name
inside the *Pride and Prejudice* cover.

Then slowly
   turn the page.

It is a truth universally acknowledged . . .

The book falls closed
   almost,

except for the second-to-last page,
which yawns
against the stub fingers
on my right hand.
There,
surrounded in hearts and flowery swirls,
are tiny handwritten words
I've never seen before. . . .

I'm too shocked to read
at first,
because how many times
have I leafed
through these pages
and missed this?

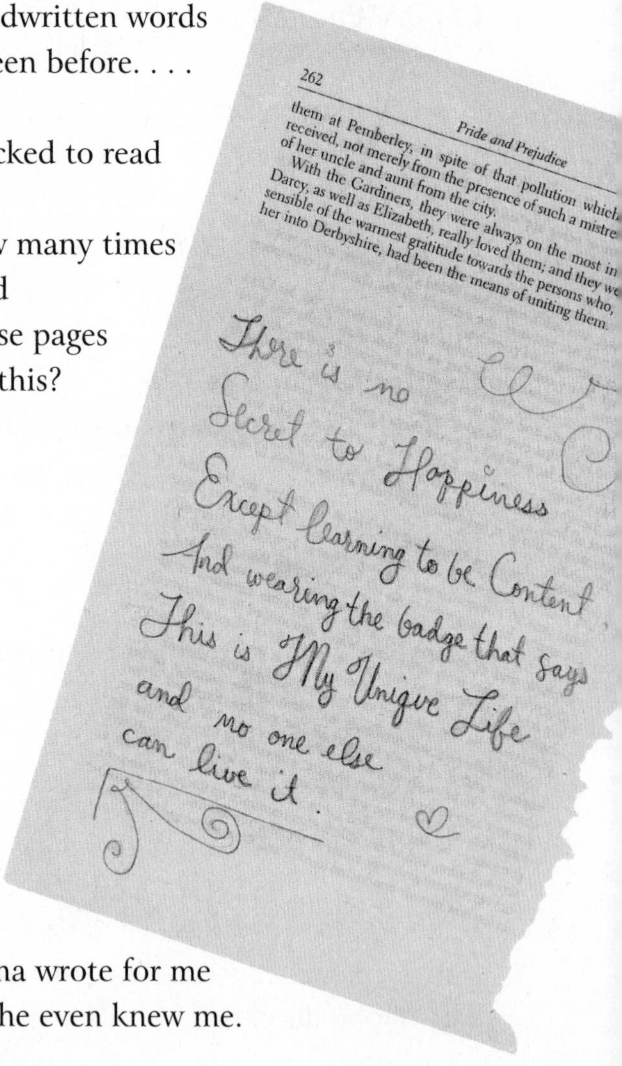
262 *Pride and Prejudice*

them at Pemberley, in spite of that pollution which
received, not merely from the presence of such a mistre
of her uncle and aunt from the city.
With the Gardiners, they were always on the most in
Darcy, as well as Elizabeth, really loved them; and they we
sensible of the warmest gratitude towards the persons who,
her into Derbyshire, had been the means of uniting them.

There is no
Secret to Happiness
Except learning to be Content
And wearing the badge that says
This is My Unique Life
and no one else
can live it.

Words Mama wrote for me
    before she even knew me.

Blue Baby

At the kitchen table
the next morning
I ask the question
that's been knocking around
in my brain,
the question I've been too afraid to ask
because I don't want to face
Em's flare of disdain.

What's a blue baby?
It's a dangerous question,
considering Em
is scowling into her cereal bowl.

Exactly what it sounds like,
she says
without looking up.
My skin was
literally
blue.
That's why my birth parents
didn't want me.

Oh, Em,
Mrs. Gurnsey says,
stirring peanut butter.
Don't say it that way.

It's the truth, isn't it?
Em shouts.
I mean,
it's a fact,
MOM.

Em scoots back her chair
and leaves,
stomping up the back stairs.

I feel the tick
of guilt
for causing trouble,
        but I push it down
because there are lots of ways
to deal with sadness.
Em doesn't have to be this way.

Then abruptly she's back,
shoving a photo album
under my nose
with a picture of a baby
in padded clothing,
hair shaved short,
sitting on a colorful nursery floor,
        lips,
        rims of fingernails
        all tinged blue,
but smiling,
hands clapping,

a short-haired
chubby
Emily.

I was cute, right?
Em says,
setting her elbows on the table.
I mean, despite the blueness?

You were cute
even with the blueness,
I say,
still shocked she came back,
but also surprised
by her smile.

We're just thankful you're okay,
Mrs. Gurnsey says,
smearing peanut butter
over a slice of bread.
We're thankful
a scar
is all you have
to remind us
you were sick.

Some days I don't like it,
Em says,
lacing
her long fingers,

the fingers I would love to have
to play the piano.
But I'm sure you don't
like having your hand
that way either.

I duck my hand
under the table.

It's okay,
Em says.
People'll get used to it,
you know.
It's too hot here
to go around in
long sleeves
all the time.

Too hot
never to go swimming, either,
I say.

Em tips her head.
You got me there.

Learning

Em teaches me a song
to play for Mama,

for when Mrs. Gurnsey
lets me open the computer again.

It has twinkly notes
up high
that I make
one by one
with my nubs of fingers

and deep notes
down low
I pound with my regular hand.

All my fingers are happy
when I play,
    even the not-quite-formed ones.

Finished

Mrs. Gurnsey scrubs
the toilet with a brush
to make the inside
bleachy clean.

I lay Mama's *Pride and Prejudice*
on the counter
next to one of the sinks.
    (They have two
    right next to each other
    so they can brush their teeth
    separately
    but together.)

I'm done,
I say.

Mrs. Gurnsey raises
her head.
Done?

With Pride and Prejudice,
I say.
Sorry I didn't let you read it with me.

That's okay.
She sits back on her haunches,
the toilet brush dangling
into the bowl.

She blinks
like waking up.
Well, congratulations.
I think we should celebrate,
maybe rent the movie
and do popcorn?

Okay.

Under the Surface

I practice piano
every day
and Mrs. Gurnsey's
smile
is a light
that starts in her eyes
and glows out her cheeks
and through the shining strands
of her hair,
falling forward
into her face
as she leans over the open lid
to watch the
piano hammers
plunk
every time
I press a note.

I think your mama in Montana
needs to hear this,
she says.

I smile,
a smile that's been
waiting
under the surface
since the music began.

Return

I return
the granola bars
two
by
two.

Mrs. Gurnsey
only says,
peering at the pile
while she makes her shopping list,
Wow, I guess I bought
a few too many granola bars.

Dreams

Next week I'm
starting piano lessons
with Emily's teacher.
I'll wear
my new sleeveless dress
    because she'll get used to
    seeing my hand
    the way it is.

Every song I learn
I'll play for Mama
through the computer.

But Mrs. Gurnsey gets to hear it
first, because
I'm getting used to her smile.

Dear Toby

Sorry it took me
    so long to say hello
    but
        (I couldn't think of you
        without the
        churning ache
        of missing).

I'm doing fine
    (now
    not before
    but now
    okay
    getting there).
The Gurnseys are nice,
their house is a mansion,
and I have my own
    (quiet)
room
with carpet
and shelves of books
and birds on the wall.

I'm learning
to play
piano
    (even with my
    stubby hand—
    it's possible!)
which is fun
    (and
    hard
    sometimes
    but
    beautiful).

I have two sisters
who are also from
China

and about my age
(though
they're as
different
from me
and different
from each other
as people
can be)
but you probably
already knew that.

Next year I'll start
seventh grade
(with three hundred
other kids
my age
who don't
know
anything
about me
and might not
like me
and I'll have
to wear short sleeves
because it will be hot
and I'll have to run
in PE)
with my sister Emily.

How is Lin Lin?
How is Yang Zi?
How is Tianjin?
Are you busy?
Say HI to everyone for me.

Sincerely,
Kara

Return Letter

On the kitchen table
lies an envelope, unopened,
with Chinese stamps!

The written words are
small, precise,
and a photo slides out
of the neatly folded paper,
a photo that sharpens the breath
in my lungs.

Dear Kara,

Fantastic to hear from you!

I found this old photo
of our
Xiao Bo
from about a year ago,
before you came to the orphanage.
I thought you would like
to have it.
It's not the same around here
without you two.

We're all doing as well
as can be expected.
Lin Lin sends
her love
and wants you to know
she's learned to roll.

Had a funny thing happen
the other day.
One of the kids
(won't mention any names)
brought me this and said
she thought it might be yours,
asked me to mail it to you.
I think she's right
because I recall seeing it
brightening your hair.

Glad the red butterfly
can find
her proper
home again.

Don't fret if the adjustment to your new life
has been tough.
Remember,
it takes a while for a butterfly's wings
to dry.

Affectionately yours,
Toby

Over My Shoulder

Pretty,
Mrs. Gurnsey says,
reaching past my shoulder
to touch the gauze
of the red butterfly's
wings.

May I?
she asks,
picking up the photograph.
Who are they?

This is Toby,
I say, pointing.
And this is—
my voice breaks—
Xiao Bo.

Mrs. Gurnsey scoots out a chair,
settles beside me.

Tell me about them,
she says.

The unsaid words
have crushed my heart.
I think
finally
it might be time
to speak them.

Epilogue

ONE YEAR LATER

Flying

I'm flying
over America
with Mom,
just the two of us,
over trees
and hills
and rivers
on our way to
Missoula,
Montana.
    (There aren't as many mountains
    as I expected.
    Maybe someday
    when I'm older
    I *will* ride my bike
    from Tampa
    to Montana
    and back again.)

I want to tell
Mama
so many things
when I see her—
    about my new red bike
    that Mom lets me
    ride to school
    and my locker
    and how I got As
    in English and art
    and how my piano teacher
    says I have a gift
    and thinks someday
    I'll play
    at Carnegie Hall.

When the plane lands
I feel the
crash
crash
of my heart,
want to dig my nails into the
armrests
because I'm really
actually here
and I didn't have to take a bus,
sneak away,
or live on granola bars.
    All I had to do was ask.

From the jetway tunnel
I catch a glimpse of them all
behind a blue dividing rope.
    My feet slow.
    Mom's hand squeezes my arm.

    Mama's hair is dyed brown,
    cut short, but
    I knew that from our screen talks.
    Daddy is all blur and scruffy cheeks,
    and Jody is thinner—
    or maybe I'm just used to looking at
    Americans.
    Matthew and Madison
    are toothy smiles
    and blue, blinking eyes.

Now my feet can't hold still.
I run
    run
        run
            and hurl myself into Mama's
            waiting arms.

Her clothes are different
    stiffer
    newer
    colorful
    scratchy
and her perfume is thick.

When I bury my face into her neck
her dangling earrings
    tickle my cheek,
the air around us filled with
    hello/oh, honey/how was your flight/this way,
words people say when there are too many words.

Through the blur,
I notice
Mom hanging back,
timid,
with a smile as fake
as the Gucci purse
from China
that hangs on her arm.

This is my new mom,
Marilyn Gurnsey,
I say in my
BIG
LOUD
MONTANA
voice
that can be heard
across mountain ranges.

Mama extracts herself
from me
and stretches out her arms.

She looks old,
but beautiful,
her face lit
with a joy
I forgot could live there,
that I only ever saw
in Hangzhou pictures.

Thank you.
Her voice whispers like a prayer
as she grips Mom's hand.

Mom's mouth opens,
but all she can do is nod.

Mama pulls her
into a long,
rocking
hug.
Then they
reach for me
and I come
to nestle between them,
caught up
in their fierce
stubborn
irrepressible
love.

Author's Note

Every author dreams of writing a book about a subject that's rooted deeply in her heart. My chance came when I wrote the book you're holding now.

I grew up in the bustling city of Hong Kong, on the southern tip of China. In those days, Hong Kong was a British colony, separate from the Chinese motherland. During my senior year of high school, I traveled with a friend over the border to Fuzhou, a city about halfway up China's coast, to teach English to college students. While on that trip we were invited to visit a local orphanage.

China formally introduced its one-child policy in 1980, which means that, since that time, most Chinese couples have only been allowed to have one baby. Families who have more than one, by accident or by choice, are heavily fined, threatened, even bullied by government agencies. Over the thirty-odd years since this law went into effect, many healthy babies have been abandoned, maybe because they had the misfortune of being born a second child, or because of their sex (boys are traditionally prized in Chinese culture over girls). Even more often, children with any kind of physical difference are left by their birth parents, sometimes at the hospital, on a street corner, or outside a government building. In China, abandoning your baby is illegal, but since parents have only one chance at raising a child, they face enormous social and family pressure to produce a "perfect" offspring.

I saw the fallout of the one-child policy for the first time when I visited the Fuzhou orphanage. The cribs in the baby room were crowded with healthy baby girls. I spent the morning holding toddlers and playing games. Later, as I passed a partially open, dark doorway, I heard a whimpering sound. It was what I found when I went through that door that changed my life forever.

I peeked into the empty room and saw a newborn wrapped up tightly in a crib near the door. He had a cleft lip, a facial difference that's fairly easy to fix with surgery, but because the orphanage staff didn't have the correct bottle to feed him, or the money for surgery, he'd been left in that dark room to die.

I was seventeen years old. I held that baby to my chest and wished I could take him home, but adoption wasn't an option. I was in high school and there was a border between my home and this orphanage, not to mention miles of red tape. I didn't know what else to do except, with many tears and prayers, lay him back in his crib and walk away.

That experience planted a seed of sorrow in my heart. I was determined to come back someday, to make a difference in a Chinese orphan's life.

Seven years later, newly married and armed with a college degree, I was back in China to work in an international school. I'd only been in China a couple weeks when I got my chance to visit the orphanage in our city of Tianjin. Conditions there were much better than in the orphanage I'd visited years before in Fuzhou, but some problems remained—too many babies and not enough help. I'd been visiting the baby room for a few weeks when a new arrival caught my eye. She had a cleft lip and palate and reminded me of that tiny baby I'd had to leave behind in Fuzhou.

I can relate to Kara's mama in this way—it felt as if God reached down and placed this tiny child in my arms. I knew we were meant to be together.

My husband and I brought that baby girl home to be ours, but, because of Chinese adoption regulations, weren't allowed to adopt her right away. We spent a total of eight wonderful years in China, working and waiting. During those years, I volunteered with an organization that worked to improve conditions at the orphanage. Throughout this book, you've heard the echoes of stories I picked up during my time as a volunteer. Kara's story is fictional, but so many real children set the precedent for her experiences. I heard of children being fostered by Western parents who were forced to leave China abruptly, of loving foster parents who had to give up their beloved children to new families, and of other families who brought abandoned children into their homes who never acquired the necessary paperwork for adoption. At the orphanage, I met children with limb differences like Kara's and debilitating cerebral palsy like Xiao Bo's and Lin Lin's. All of these stories went into a melting pot to make Kara who she is.

Our own story ended happily. After six and a half years of fostering our daughter, we were finally able to adopt. We now live in the United States, but fondly remember our years in the amazing country of China. I feel enormously fortunate to be able to share a story set in a place, among a people, and about a subject so very precious to me.

Acknowledgments

Thank you, God,

for all your gifts, including this one.

Thank you, Aaron,

for loving me, for giving me writing time, for your listening ear.

Thank you, sweet children of mine, all of you,

for your hugs and kisses, for all your enthusiasm.

Thank you, Mom,

for giving me a unique view of the world, for always encouraging my writing.

Thank you, Dad,

for long walks and talks, for helping me find my True North.

Thank you, Michelle and Steve,

for shaping, inspiring, pushing me.

Thank you, Nai Nai and Papa,

for love and support in so many ways.

Thank you, critique partners and cheerleaders, Christa, Caroline, Grace, Janet, Jesalyn, Julie, Krista, Kristin, Melissa, Melodie, and the Sub Club,

for being amazing writers in your own rights, for sharing your gifts with me.

Thank you, Maliya, Jimmy, Rosalie and Megan,

for your beautiful, sometimes-painful, always-hopeful stories.

Thank you, Papa, Kim, Patrick and Kimberly,
for your support and expertise.

Thank you, Mid-Columbia Gymnastics Academy,
for giving me "office space" on the sidelines, for letting me use your electricity and your bathroom.

Thank you, Kate,
for crying when you read my work, for believing in me, for finding this book a home.

Thank you, Amy June Bates, for your gorgeous artwork
that made this story come alive.

Thank you, Christian and the amazing team at Simon & Schuster,
for loving this novel, for pouring your hearts into making it a beautiful, real book.